The Medallion

W. C. Dick

I would like to thank my wife Cheryl for allowing me to follow my dreams even when they have taken me far away from her. I would also like to thank the many friends who read what I had written and pushed me toward publication. I would like to also thank Edie without whose help the GPS portion of this book would not have been possible.

Preface

Parts of this book had been floating around in my head for some time when I walked into a second hand store and saw the medallion. It was exactly as Jase found it in the story. That find was the catalyst for moving this story from the depths of my mind to the written form you now have. This story is a work of fiction, but I have taken great pains to keep it as historically and physically accurate as possible. This is a story not of what happened, but of what might have happened.

Students of History may find it interesting to try and identify the unit he was serving with in the war, or perhaps do their own research on the Indian battles mentioned. Those familiar with building of the transcontinental railroad might understand from the last words in the book one of the places my mind might be taking me for perhaps another book.

It is my hope that this book can in some way trigger in others an interest in travel and/or history so they might find even a small amount of the enjoyment I found while writing it. Toward that end I have included a guide that may work as a start to pique one's interest to get off the couch and see some of this great country.   Wayne

CHAPTER 1

The rider stopped as he came to the edge of the hills overlooking Lake De Smet, Dakota Territory. He sat quietly on the black horse as his shaded eyes scanned the terrain with his ears tuned for any sound. The black stood as still as his rider, alert not only to his surroundings, but also for any slight indication from its rider. In the few months they had been together, the communication bonds between horse and rider had built to a point where an observer could not see any sign pass between them. Yet any warning from the horse's keen senses seem to go directly to the rider as easily as the horse could perceive any command from the rider as though reading his mind. The sorrel pack horse stood quietly, awaiting any signal from either the other horse or the rider.

Observing no movement, other than an eagle soaring slowly in search of prey, the rider dismounted taking his compacted telescope out of a small bag on the side of the saddle and his rifle from its scabbard. Leaving the reins looped around the horn of the saddle so the black would not step on them if he had to move fast, the rider ascended to a clump of brush on the point of a hill.

Taking off his flat brimmed hat so it would not show an unnatural silhouette against the broad expanse of blue sky, he slipped amongst the brush. With his buckskin shirt and brown trousers blending well with the background, he found a place where the brush behind him was slightly above his head before he sat down. Here, with his shoulder length brown hair and thick beard doing the job of blending his tanned white face into the background brush, he could study the valley unobserved.

Extending the telescope, he checked out the valley carefully. There were deer, antelope and a small heard of buffalo, but the only sign of humans was what appeared to be an Indian encampment far across the lake. The distance was so great that even with the telescope he could not be sure.

Due to Indian hostilities, he had been moving quite carefully since he had left the army column a few days back. The column was part of the contingent assigned to capture Sioux Indians that had been forced westward after the uprising in Minnesota the year before. He was reasonably sure the small group that had been following his trail the last four days were some of the Sioux working their way west after skirmishes with the army and settlers around the Missouri River.

He had decided, after the first couple of days, that the Indians were not trying to catch up with him, but followed his trail only because of convenience and opportunity. The trails he had used had provided reasonably good travel westward and the prints of his shod horses promised the possible opportunity to gain goods, horses, and a scalp. Moving at a steady yet cautious pace, he had stayed from three to five hours ahead of them which led him to believe they were using caution with their movements as well. He estimated that, due to the lateness of the day, it would be well after dark before the Indians could travel the distance they would have to come to reach the lake. Adding to that the availability of a good camp area along a stream some distance back, it would be very unlikely they would enter the area today. With this in mind, he decided he would try to find himself a good camping spot along the shore for the night. A slight smile crossed his face at the thought of a possible catch of fish to supplement his tasteless diet of the last few days.

Catching his weight with his left arm when he slipped as he was descending the slope, he winced at the pain. Unconsciously rubbing the twisted arm, he cussed the bullet that had shattered it. He had worked with the arm until he had almost normal usage of it, but movement would sometimes cause a stab of pain. This stab of pain would cause him to wince, and his body to jerk, so he had learned not to trust the arm when doing things requiring steadiness. His right arm, however, seemed to have learned to compensate for many of the lacking abilities of the left. This gain was not due to any conscious thought on his part, but seemed to come naturally as he regained lost strength from the weakened condition he was in after his escape from the prison camp. Leaving these thoughts behind, he mounted the waiting black and rode down to the lake.

As the rider was following a well used trail along the shore looking for an area in which to camp, he came to a place where the main trail turned sharply away from the shore of the lake. The trail he was on seemed to continue along the shore, but from this point it showed no recent usage, except for animals. The main traffic went away from the lake and appeared to be circling around the area ahead of him. Studying the area, and seeing no visible reason for the detour, curiosity won out and he continued along the unused trail.

Riding a few yards into the area, he came to a place that seemed to be ideal for a camp. It appeared to be adequately defendable with a grassy sheltered area for the horses. Careful observation showed the scattered bones of what appeared to be five or six coyotes, but no reason for the lack of usage or avoidance. Having found no reason against it, he picketed his horses and setup a comfortable camp. Within fifteen minutes of digging out the fishing string he carried, and mixing up some dough for making fry bread and to use for bait, he had three nice sized trout for supper. Building a concealed fire out of dry wood, so neither fire nor smoke would be easily visible, he prepared the best meal he had eaten for some time.

All the while he had been struggling to fill in the gaps of a half remembered story that he had heard while trading with some of the Indians on the reservations in Minnesota. While eating, the gaps finally filled in and he felt he knew the reason for the lack of travel in this spot. The Indians believed the area to be a place of evil spirits and death.

So the story goes: A sizable Blackfoot raiding party, traveling south of their normal lands, had caught up with an old, white haired trapper and pinned him down by a big water. The battle had lasted three days, with five of the Indians being killed and four more wounded. Finally killing the trapper, the Indians took what they could use of his belongings and one of the warriors took his scalp. While the warrior was dancing around, displaying the white haired scalp lock, he suddenly fell dead. During the same night, some coyotes ravaged the body and the rest of the dead trapper's belongings.

The next morning the Indians found the coyotes lying dead a short distance away. The Indians gathered their dead and left, leaving the scalp lock lay where it had fallen. Two or three of the Indians, who had possession of things that had belonged to the old trapper, also died suddenly over the next few days. The Indians burned and then buried the remains of the things they had taken from the old trapper and had no further unexplained deaths after. They then spread the word about the evil in that place to all they encountered. Thus the story became well known and the area became known as a place of death and evil. Being quite certain he had found the place of the story, the rider decided to spend some time the next day to see if he could find and bury the old trapper's remains.

He awoke early the next day, caught a couple more fish for breakfast, and began a search of the area. Starting near the remains of the coyotes, he began working around the outer edge of the area. He had checked the outer perimeter, and worked along the shore almost back to his camp, when he saw the Indians coming out of the hills. Taking his rifle, he checked and moved his horses before working in areas where he could keep out of sight yet watch the movements of the Indians.

There were seven braves mounted on good ponies and leading three pack animals. They looked to be Sioux, as he had suspected, but none were sporting war paint. They came along the same trail he had taken until they came to the fork where he had split off from the well traveled trail. Here they dismounted and had an animated discussion while observing his tracks into the forbidden area. Due to both he and his horses being out of sight they knew only that he had entered the area, but did not know if he was still there.

Moving back down the trail a short distance they set about making a small camp. Two of the braves mounted their ponies and headed out on the trail that circled the area. Three went about gathering dry wood and built a fire while the remaining two braves walked separately along the shore and then moved a few feet into the water. He guessed that the two braves that had ridden off were circling the area looking for sign to determine whether he had exited the area on the far side or was still nearby so should be no cause for concern. Being intrigued by the actions of the two braves in the lake, the rider lay quietly in his cover and watched those still left. The braves in the lake were both in knee deep water moving very carefully in a bent position with the hand away from shore held in the water. With a sudden movement, one of the braves swooped a fair sized fish over onto the shore. This was followed by woops of approval by those in the camp.

By the time the scouts returned from their sojourn around the area the others had thirteen fish cooking on the fire. Six caught by the brave that had caught the first fish and seven by the other. Now the second fisherman was getting the approval of the group with the other being playfully scorned. Seated around the fire, eating their meal of fish, the rest received the report of the scouts and discussed the situation with much questioning in the direction of the hidden rider. The discussion became quite heated at times as there seemed to be differing ideas as to moving on or staying. One big brave that was wearing an army coat, and who seemed to be the leader, was very concerned with the rider. He kept making signs toward the tracks the rider had left and the area he was in. Finally the discussion broke up and they began setting up a more permanent camp. Now it was the rider's turn to make some decisions.

By the Indians actions, he was sure of two things. One was that he was indeed in the area in which the old trapper had died and that was believed to be an evil place by the Indians. The other was that they were more interested in him than their destination. He had no idea what their plans might be, but he was quite sure they would not challenge the evil spirits by entering the area, at least for the time being. If they stayed camped where they were it would be reasonably easy for him to slip out of the other side of the area, though he might have to wait until dark. Even if they posted a guard along the trail he would have little trouble as both horses were used to moving silently when the situation dictated. The only problem with leaving was that he had not found the old trapper's body and laid him to rest, and for some unknown reason, he could not ride away from that chore.

He had told himself that putting distance between himself and the Sioux was the smart thing to do. He would probably not be able to

11

find the old trapper's remains anyway. Some other trapper or traveler had probably already found them and done him the service, or his bones all may have been carried off by the scavengers of the wild. Reason as much as he could, however, he could not bring himself to leave the area without at least making an effort to find the remains and do the old trapper justice. The decision made, he decided he best try to find out what the Indians intended.

The Indians knew where he was but had not seen him yet, so he would let them lay an eyeball on their quarry. He decided to go fishing. Taking his rifle in one hand and fishing line in the other he walked to the lake shore. When he stepped into view the Indian camp came alive. Surprised by his sudden appearance, they jumped to their feet, all talking at once and pointing his way. Wishing he had white hair and beard like the old trapper, he almost laughed out loud at the thought of what their reactions might be had they thought he was the ghost of the old man. He sat down within view, but mostly hidden by the trunk of an old tree that had fallen partially in the water. Though he doubted their accuracy with their old smooth-bore guns that he had seen as he had watched them through his telescope, he did not wish to chance a lucky shot, if they were so inclined. Not receiving immediate hostile action, the rider found he was enjoying the relaxation of just sitting in the warm sun waiting for the fish to bite. He was so comfortable it was almost an inconvenience to haul in a fish when one would take his line.

After about an hour, he took his catch and walked to the hollowed out area where he had his fire. Stopping part way, he looked directly at the Indian camp so there would be no question that he was aware of them before continuing on out of sight to his fire pit. Stirring the coals he found some that were still hot. Adding some dry twigs, and blowing on them, he soon had a good cooking fire going. After a supper of fish and fry bread he decided there was enough time before dark to continue scouting around for the remains. The Indian camp seemed to be quiet and no attempts had been made to enter the area nor were any other signs of aggression shown. Quite relaxed with the situation, he took up his rifle and began to methodically search a higher, more centered section of the area. At times this would put him in full view of the Indian camp. As he went up one small rise giving a good view of the whole area, a bullet whizzed by a short distance away followed by the crack of the rifle.

His reaction was to dive flat on his stomach between two rotting tree trunks. Moving to a kneeling position, he peered over one of the trunks toward the Indian camp. The braves were all looking toward his position, with one holding a rifle. There was still a trace of the black powder smoke from the old muzzle loader hanging in the air. He slipped the barrel of his rifle over the log with his right hand, took aim, and sent an answering shot inches over their heads. He did not intend to hit any of them. The shot was intended only to let them know he was alive and well. As he watched them scatter on the ground he made a mental note about being more careful as he moved around so as not to be as much of a temptation for a shot.

After he settled down from the fast movement of the short exchange, he looked more closely at his position. It was a good position to defend with room to move and good shelter all around, except for one small gap facing the lake. This would be the place to be if the situation escalated into a fight. He would bring some water up, fill the gap with rocks and perhaps sleep here tonight after he checked on his horses again. He then vaguely remembered a hollow clunk as his rifle struck something when he dove into the shelter. He checked the rifle for damage, and upon finding none, he then looked around the log by which he had landed when he entered. There, partially under an overhang of the log, was the upper portion of a skull. Some white hair was still intact, but the lower jaw was missing. He had found the old trapper.

The significance of this did not register with him though, as the sight of the skull had taken him back to the horrors of war. His mind was seeing the face of a Union solder with staring dead eyes, and lower jaw shot away. Along with this came the memory of the pain he had felt in both his head and arm. These were the sensations that had greeted him as he regained consciousness among the dead and dying scattered about that bloody field of battle. He fought to control his thoughts and dismiss those of the war still raging in the East. Deciding not to disturb the old trapper until the morrow, he saw that the Indian camp was preparing for the night and set about his own needs. He checked and talked to his horses, banked the fire for the next morning, carried water up and moved his gear to the shelter of the logs. Checking his weapons, and after one last check of the Indian camp, he settled in for a restless night's sleep.

CHAPTER 2

Awakening early, the rider again checked the Indian camp. Seeing nothing amiss, he set about making breakfast. Moving to his fire pit, he kindled a fire and put on some coffee. Due to limits imposed by carrying his rifle with him as he moved around the camp, he had to make another trip to his gear for some bacon to fry with the remainder of his fish. The Indians appeared to be cooking breakfast also as he could see them milling around their fire. He put the fish and bacon at the edge of the fire, poured a cup of coffee, and sitting where he had a good view of the Indian camp, began to ponder the possible challenges of the day.

He was sure most of the old trapper's remains would be in the sheltered area covered partially by the blown sand that had accumulated since his demise, so burial should be easy, though time consuming. He also wanted to examine the area for any scraps left of the old trapper's gear that might shed some light on whom he was, and that would take even more time. Of main concern though, was that he did not know the intent of his Indian neighbors. If they left, he should have time to accomplish his goals and leave the area before they could collect enough braves to return and pin him there. If they did happen to return before he left, it would be only a matter of time until he joined the old trapper by means of either starvation or a bullet.

As he rose to check his breakfast, a bullet kicked up dirt scant inches away. Diving for cover, and grabbing his rifle as he went, he saw the smoke from a muzzleloader dissipating in the air above a clump of brush. Keeping his head low, he changed position to a more sheltered spot before surveying the area. At the Indian camp there was much chatter and pointing toward his camp. All the Indians could be accounted for except the one in the army coat. Closely observing the brush by which he had seen the smoke, he caught a quick glint of sun on metal as something moved behind the brush.

The brush was located along the trail skirting the forbidden area. It was over two hundred yards away and he gained new respect for the Indian's shooting ability. Keeping low, he retrieved his now mostly burnt breakfast from the fire and ate it while watching the brush with occasional glances at the Indian camp. The other Indians sat around eating while watching the ensuing drama. Occasional glances in the direction of the brush by the other Indians led him to believe Army Coat was still there. However, as closely as he had watched the brush, he had seen no sign of the Indian other than that first glint.

After about thirty minutes of waiting, he decided to open this shindig up and see if he could force the Indian's hand. Holding aim slightly above the area where he had earlier seen the glint, he squeezed off a round. He then followed it with two other shots, one to the left and one to the right, as fast as he could lever shells into the chamber of the Henry repeater. He was rewarded by a surprised retort and returning shot that went wild. Shortly, he caught a glimpse of the blue coat disappearing into a low spot in the earth where none seemed to be.

He was amazed at the Indians' abilities to work with the land to become invisible in places of little, or no, seeming shelter. Within minutes, he spotted Army Coat back in the camp, though he had not seen him enter. Pouring a cup of what by now was very strong coffee, the rider moved to the sheltered area where his gear was stashed and the bones of the old trapper lay. Digging out a few inches of the blown sand, toward one end of the shelter, supplied a place for him to stand at full height and just see over the trunks that were supplying protection. While digging he had the added good fortune of finding what appeared to be a leg bone, which he placed aside. As he worked, he kept a close eye on the Indian camp making a head count every few minutes.

The rider had felt the Indians would either leave the area themselves, or wait until he left the area before making any earnest attempt to kill him, but this did not seem to be the case. The shot taken by Army Coat from the brush was proof that at least he wanted him dead. He could not understand why Army Coat was so intent on killing him when the Indians had shown such reluctance to enter the forbidden area. They could not gain his horses, belongings or scalp without the gamble of offending the evil spirits.

Trying to think the situation over from an Indian point of view, he could think of only two possible reasons. The first was that because of constant repression from whites, and the probable loss of family to white guns and disease, Army Coat had built such hatred toward whites that he was obsessed with seeing all whites dead. The other possibility stemmed from some Indians belief that when you kill an enemy you gain the power and strength of that enemy. Army coat may believe that, if he kills the rider, whatever medicine the rider possesses that allows him to dwell among the evil spirits unharmed would transfer to him. With this power, Army Coat would be able to enter the area to collect his booty without fear of death by the spirits of the area. Whatever the reason, the attempt on his life had narrowed the rider's options.

The rider had taken the Sharps Fifty-two from where he kept it wrapped in his gear. He wiped it down and laid out a dozen rounds. The Indians had shown they had no intentions of moving on and leaving him be. Consequently, he could not continue with the work he had to do with the constant threat of taking a bullet at any time he happened to give an opportunity. He held no remorse for these men and did not wish to kill them. He had seen Indians cheated, mistreated, and killed as the white man moved to take over their land and he could not blame them for their hatred of the whites. He could comprehend their plight as not only their land but also their way of life was being taken from them. Was not his reasoning when he elected to fight in the war much the same? He was himself fighting against oppression and the dictation of how he was to live and think.

He had seen too much death and killing on the battlefields, which was a major part of his decision to drift west. He was tired of the killing and had hopes of avoiding trouble, but the Indians persistence seemed to leave no alternative. He was confident of his abilities and the accuracy of the Sharps at seeming amazing ranges, so he would do what he had to do. If he was right in his estimation of the distance to the Indian camp, and he was sure he was, Army Coat would die with the first heavy bullet. One other brave, who seemed to side with Army Coat on decisions involving him, would die also. The others would have the chance to ride away. If they did not, time and providence would dictate the outcome. Army Coat was standing facing him while speaking to the others, presenting himself as a perfect target. He slid a linen cartridge into the chamber of the Sharps, and set the primer. Adjusting the sight, he settled his aim on the single button holding the front of the coat together and eased pressure on the set trigger.

All of a sudden, a brave jumped to his feet blocking the shot and the rider quickly released the trigger. The brave was gesturing and pointing beyond Army Coat. The reason for the excitement was a small herd of Buffalo drifting slowly out of a fold in the hills about a thousand yards away. This small herd may provide an opportunity to avoid the battle he was about to start. If he could drop one of the buffs, it would have the dual purpose of showing the danger of attacking against a weapon with such long-range accuracy and show friendship through a present of food to the Indians.

Adjusting the sight on the Sharps to its highest position, which was eight hundred yards, he steadied himself for the shot. Placing the weapon in the notch he had made in the log to supply added support for his previously intended shot, he set the sights above the head of a big bull about even with the top of the hump. If his estimation of the distance was right, and his adjustment for the slight breeze blowing in across the lake, the heavy fifty two-caliber bullet should explode the heart causing instant death. Squeezing the set trigger, he moved his finger to the firing trigger. Taking a breath and easing it slowly out he applied slight pressure to the trigger. With a roar, the sharps bucked against his shoulder. At the crack of the rifle and the whine of the bullet passing overhead, the Indians, who had been watching the Buffalo, dove to the ground and scrambled for cover. He barely saw the dust kick up under the heavy chest of the bull. He had missed.

Other than raising his head from his

grazing and looking around, the bull hardly moved. Realizing he had under estimated the distance, the rider slipped another round into the chamber and readied another shot. The Indians, unsure if he was shooting at them or the buffalo, watched both he and the buffs from their cover. Aiming slightly higher, but using the same windage, the rider squeezed off another shot. Though taking only seconds, it seemed to take forever for the heavy bullet to reach its target. As the bullet hit, the bull gave a slight hump of his back, his legs folded, and he dropped straight down. Having the range now, the rider also dropped a younger, smaller bull a short distance from the first. Moving out of his shelter so he could be plainly seen, he pointed at the buffalo, at the Indians, and back toward the buffalo. With the Indians just starting to comprehend and watching him with awe, he turned and walked to the less sheltered area of his fire.

As full realization came, the Indians mounted their ponies, and leading their packhorses, headed to the buffalo. In a short while, one of the braves rode back into their camp with cuts of meat tied across his pony. He stirred the coals and got a good fire going before stringing some of the buffalo meat above it. He then lashed two small logs together and tied some of the meat to them. Walking to the edge of the forbidden area, he went a short distance into the lake. Checking the direction of the breeze, he pushed hard on the logs sending the small raft further into the lake. He then returned to his cooking and turned the meat over the fire.

At first, the rider thought sending the raft of meat into the lake was some sort of ceremonial gesture for the spirits. As he watched the breeze slowly turn the little raft toward shore, he realized the meat was meant for him. It was an ingenious way of sharing the bounty without entering the evil area. In a short while, the raft was bumping against the fallen tree he had used for shelter while fishing. Shortly after that, he was drinking coffee while the meat simmered over the fire.

A short time later, the rest of the Indians returned with the meat and hides loaded on their pack animals. They spent a couple of hours gorging on the buffalo meat and talking. It never failed to amaze him how much the Indian could eat at one setting, and how long they could go without food if necessary. There had been occasions he had gone long times without food, but he could not begin to pack in the amount of food he had seen them eat. After they finished eating, the Indians proceeded to pack up their camp.

When they were about finished, Army Coat put choice cuts of the meat into a large bag that appeared to be made out of a type of canvas that could have come from a tent or wagon cover. As the others mounted their ponies to leave, he put the bag on his pony and walked to the edge of the evil area. The rider, holding his rifle across his chest, rose to full view facing the Indian. The Indian dropped the bag of meat on the ground, pointed to it and then the rider. He then pointed to his eyes and then to the rider to tell the rider he would recognize him if they met again. As their eyes met over the distance, the Indian brought his closed fist twice to his chest. The rider did the same. A gesture of friendship, they would fight no more. Mounting his pony, the Indian turned his back, rode to his waiting companions and they all started down the trail leading away from the rider and the forbidden area.

With the threat of the Indians gone, the rider retrieved the meat Army Coat had left and set about digging out the blown sand in search of the old trapper's remains. The blow sand was easy to dig in with just his hands, but he would have to use the old axe he carried to loosen the harder ground when he buries the remains. He wished he had a shovel, but the old axe would work well enough.

Though the bones had been scattered around the pit of the shelter, most of the body was seemingly there. He had collected many of the old trapper's bones, and was digging near the spot where the skull had been when his fingers hooked something. A small piece of blue rock and metal chain became visible. He knew even before he unearthed the rest, that it was Big Jake's medicine stone. Moisture came into his eyes and heaviness filled his heart as he realized the bones belonged to the big man who had taught him so much. Perhaps, deep in his being, he had suspected the white haired trapper was his old friend and that had been the reason he had felt so strongly the need to lay his bones to rest. Many thoughts of the old man filled his mind as he reverently examined the medallion Jake had called his Medicine Stone.

The Medallion was a circle of blue stone, about two inches across, encased in a gold ring. Fastened to the ring was a necklace made of two strands, which hooked together at the ends to accommodate removal. Each strand was made of wire loops with blue stones on each loop. Twenty-six of the stones, thirteen on each strand, are cylindrical and, according to Jake, kept him in contact with the spirits of thirteen brave men. Six of the loops, three each side, contained what to Jase looked like six-petal flowers. Jake had told him they were a representation of the outward flow of the strength contained within each living creature.

The Medallion itself was etched with three double-lined circles with a face like etching contained within the center circle. This face depicted a being with a prominent nose, high cheekbones and a v-shaped mouth extending to the chin. Jake explained this as being The Creator, or Great Spirit, within the three worlds, or heavens. Between the center and middle circles were points indicating the four directions and four dots, one dot each side of north and one each side of south. The dots, according to Jake, show a drawing of power toward these directions. Between the middle and outer ring are patterns of points and swirls in the four directions depicting the four winds and the power contained within them. At the places where the four directions meet there are solidly etched points with marks underneath stretching from wind to wind. As Jake had pointed out these, he had stressed strength in flexibility and compromise.

Those things he remembered as he stared at the medallion in his hand. The medallion now had a piece broken out and missing. The missing piece was the upper left portion of the outer circle. A chill ran down the rider's spine as he realized this would be west by north, as Jake had always been drawn in these directions during his travels. In addition, when compared to the rider's home where he first met Jake, it was the direction where Jake left this world. Though he suspected the piece had been missing long before Jake had hidden the medallion in that hole beneath the log, he watched carefully for any sign of the piece as he sifted the remaining small section of sand. This proved out right, as all he uncovered were a few more bones, small scraps of what looked like dried skin with a bit of a waxy substance on it, and chip of shinny black stone with the same substance attached.

Digging deeper into the more solid earth of the shelter, he laid Jake's bones to rest in the place where the old trapper had fallen. After quoting some passages from the Bible and speaking some words to the spirit of his old friend, he committed the bones to Mother Earth. He covered the grave with the earth he had dug out and then with the blow sand until it looked much the same as when he found it. Though he did not want to actually mark the grave itself as it might be disturbed, he felt compelled to lash together a small cross out of twigs which he placed on a rise a few feet away. No name, just a marker to acknowledge the passing of a life. Making some coffee and something to eat, he sat to mourn his friend and make plans to continue on his way west.

As he ate his mind supplied visual pictures of Jake in times past. He saw him sitting on a rock in his buckskin clothes talking of places far away. He saw him in the borrowed suit, which was a bit too small, that he had worn when Paw and Olga had talked him into going to that social down in the valley. However, no matter how he viewed the old man, two things were always present. Jake always wore the medallion and had his possibles bag hooked on his belt. His pouch of life and death, he had called it. The bag had items essential to survival such as fire starting equipment, rawhide strips for making snares and binding together shelter and his death box. The death box! The rider hadn't thought of the death box. He jumped up and retrieved the piece of black rock he had found. Scraping off some of the waxy substance he smiled at the realization of the reason for the unexplained deaths that had marked this area as a place of evil.

Jake had spent some time on the

African continent with some natives who tipped their arrows with a special poison. This poison was first made into a fine powder that was kept in sealed containers until it was ready for use. If kept sealed the mixture would last indefinitely, but if left unsealed the poison would lose potency over time. The Natives would take a small amount of the powder, and add water to make a paste that they would apply to the tip of their arrows and spears. If the arrow so much as broke the skin of an animal or human, they were dead within seconds. Only certain people were allowed to make the poison and apply it to the arrows and spears as it could cause death by simple contact if one made a mistake. Sweat would activate the poison, which would then enter the body through the skin causing eventual death.

Jake carried some of this poison with him in his death box. the rider had never seen the actual container as it was wrapped in a cover made of intestine that was coated and sealed with a wax that Jake said was made from tree sap. He said the yellow-white powder was in a box made of a type of rock soft enough to be shaped by rubbing. The same wax used on the outer bundle sealed the lid. When he had asked Jake why he carried it, the old man just answered: "Don't know, just figure I might have need of it someday". the rider spoke as if to answer the spirit of the old man, "Well Jake, I reckon you found a need."

What happened, the rider decided, was that Jake knew he was dying from his multiple wounds and did not want to be captured and perhaps tortured before he finally succumbed. He removed the medallion and covered it in the hole under the log so it would not be found. He did not want an enemy to have his medicine. He then opened the death box, probably breaking off the chip while doing so, and sprinkled the powder over his head and clothing. Knowing that as he did so, the second the poison entered one of his wounds he would gain instant death and any person that mutilated his body would soon follow due to their contact with the poison. The rider laughed with Jake's spirit as he realized how well the old trapper's final act of defiance had worked.

As the rider finished his meal and prepared to leave the forbidden area, his thoughts went back to when he first met Jake and all that had transpired since then. Sometimes he was quietly emerged in his thoughts, while at others he talked aloud to his horses. Life had changed much during those years.

CHAPTER 3

The boy saw the horses as they started down the trail into the small valley. He could make out a rider on the lead horse and the other appeared to be a pack animal. Losing sight of them as the trail dipped behind some trees, he headed toward the other side of the house. The rhythmic sound of a hammer on steel rang loudly until the boy reached the side of the man working at a rock forge. As they talked, the man walked over, picked up a rifle standing in the corner of the open shed, and moved it closer to where he was working. The boy ran back around to the front side of the house and positioned himself comfortably in a place where he could watch the trail leading into the yard.

As the horses and rider came into view, the boy ran to the back of the house and alerted the man at the forge. The man picked up the rifle and followed the boy around the house. They were sitting in the shade of the porch as the horses and rider entered the yard. Both horses were paints, but with very different markings, and looked to be of good stock. The man was quite large and dressed fully in buckskin, except for his wide brimmed hat.

Little of the face could be made out under the shadow of the hat, only a white beard with a red tint. He carried his rifle over the pommel of the saddle, not threatening, but easily at hand. Speaking with an accent strange to the boy, a gruff, but friendly voice said "I be looking for the diggings of Jamie Richards, and I ave erd it might be ere abouts."

At the sound of the voice, the man in the shade of the porch said, "Light and set Jake, you've found him." The two men met in the yard with a grin, handshake and a pat on the back. Watching the two men, the boy realized that this was the friend of which his father had spoken so highly. "An this must be your lad Jason," Jake said, as he shook the boy's hand. "Jason Jakob Richards, but they call me Jase," the boy answered, "I was named for you according to pa." Leaving Jase to help Jake unsaddle his horses and stow his gear, Jamie returned to work on the door hinges that he was making while the forge was still hot.

This was the time the rider first met Jakob Jorgenson and first saw his medallion. Jake stayed with them for nigh on six months, always making sure he did more than his share of the work around the place. During free time, Jamie and Jake talked some about their experiences in the past, but mostly caught each other up on their lives after they went separate ways.

Jake knew that Jase's mother, Katrina, had died from pneumonia a short time after Jase was born. The letter Jamie had written informing him of her death caught up with him two years later. Three other letters Jamie had written had never found Jake. On the other hand, Jake was able to keep Jamie better informed due to Jamie settling on this place shortly after he and Katrina were married, thus giving them a permanent address.

The one bit of news Jake had not written about, but decided to bring in person, was that his dead sister's only daughter, Olga, and her husband, Sven, had moved to this country. They had settled about three days ride from here and were part of the reason Jake had allowed himself to drift east. Jake, having little tolerance for rules imposed by others, and feeling crowded when living among most people, preferred life in the open country of the west.

He had found that most who lived out there, including the bulk of Indian tribes, were more focused in living with the land rather than possessing and changing it. You could see the sadness in Jake's face though, as he talked about how things were changing as more people moved into the unsettled area. So many people had little respect for the land, and the animals living on it. They killed animals for no reason other than sport, or profit, and claimed possession of large areas of land, most often more than they needed. As had happened in the east, the Indians were being forced off their traditional hunting grounds and their means of living were being wiped out. Because of this oppression, formerly friendly tribes were fast becoming enemies.

Jase learned much during Jake's stay. Jake and Jase tended to the gardening and hunting, along with working on general upkeep around the place. Jamie worked mostly at the forge building the iron products that he sold to supply needed money. Both Jake and Jase would help where they could, but neither possessed the skill required for good blacksmith work. Some free time was set aside each day for teaching, games, and talking.

Though Jamie had taught Jase at a young age, to shoot a rifle, and throw the crude tomahawk that he had made for him, they had worked little together at these things and Jase's skills were quite lacking. Working with the two men as they competed against each other, however, greatly improved his skills. He also learned to throw a knife, shoot a pistol and do well in hand to hand combat. The latter fighting done with both knife and hawk, as well as without weapons.

Jake won over half the competitions between he and Jamie, though the final tally was rather close. This bothered Jase, as he had great faith in his father. Jake, sensing the problem, told Jase that had not always been so. In days past, Jake stated, he could seldom best Jamie, and he still knew of none other he would rather have beside him if the going got rough during a fight. Jake reckoned that living a more sheltered life had robbed Jamie of some of the fighter's edge he had gained during his former challenges. Jase promised himself that he would continue working with his father after Jake was gone, so no more of that edge was lost.

Though Jake had told Jase the story surrounding his death box, explained the medallion, and talked about some of his and Jamie's other exploits, the man said little about the time they had spent together before Jamie and Katrina came to these mountains. This reluctance stemmed from Jamie's insistence that the less Jase knew of that time, the safer he and others would be. All Jase could glean from either man was that they had been involved in some type of major fight in which many had died, including those memorialized by the stones on Jake's medallion. The medallion itself was made by some type of priest or medicine man, and was given as appreciation for services rendered.

The joining of Jamie and Katrina took place during that time, and had something to do with the fight, but Jase did not know what. He did find out that Jamie and Katrina were believed dead by both sides and that belief had helped bring about the end of the fighting. Both men stressed on Jase that if the knowledge that Katrina had lived and had a son ever reached the wrong ears, many others would die. The buried past must remain buried.

When Jake decided it was time for him to leave, Jamie and Jase accompanied him as far as his niece Olga's place. When they arrived, it was quite evident that Jake looked upon her much as he would his own daughter. As she watched him playing with her two young sons, Olga laughed and talked about the good times she had with Jake before he left the old country. By enlisting Jamie's help, Olga was even able to persuade Jake to attend a social down at the settlement.

Out of respect for meeting Jake's kin,

Jamie and Jase had brought "city clothes" with them, but Olga had to borrow a neighbor's "Sunday-go-to-meeting" suit for Jake. When he put it on, the old man was really a sight. The suit was a tight fit, and a little short in the arms and legs. Jake's wide brimmed hat was replaced with a small brimmed bolo and he wore his good, beaded moccasins. Adding to this, Jake refused to leave his grungy and well-worn possibles bag, which he wore around his waist. The blue medallion also looked out of place as it hung below the black bow tie, but Jake was ready to go.

Despite Jake's confiding in Jase that he felt as out of place as a tumbleweed in a field of daises, the social went reasonably well for a while. There was some snickering about Jake's appearance, but most of these were out of his hearing. There were a couple of times gents who had partaken of too much corn squeezing got a little loud with remarks that started to get the old man's dander up. However, out of respect for Olga and because of some fear of the havoc the old man might cause were he to cut loose, others were quick to quell the men's obnoxious behavior.

Four brothers, big strapping fellows who were well known for their brawling abilities, finally pushed Jake beyond his limits. Jake said," You fellas jus give me a minute and we'll discuss this properly, don't want to mess up these ere borrod duds." With that said, he proceeded to remove the borrowed clothes. Disregarding the snickers and embarrassed actions of the ladies, and guffaws from the men, he placed the clothing in a neat pile with the bolo on top. Handing Jase his possibles bag, and medallion, this left him standing in only his worn red long johns and beaded moccasins, as he faced the brothers.

Jamie quietly removed his coat in preparation for the fight he could see was coming, but Jake raised a hand toward him and said, "Doen reckon I'll need no hep, jus gonna give these fellas a little educatin on proper mannerisms." The older brother spit in his hands as he stepped toward Jake, looking up just as the nimble old man kicked him in the face. Jake followed this with a right cross that drove the big man to his knees. Seeing their brother go down, the other three charged.

Throwing the first to reach him with a hip lock, Jake spun his leg around and swept the feet from under another. As the third bulled into him, Jake went to his back as he grabbed the man's shirt. Using the momentum built by the charge and a foot planted in the mid-section, Jake propelled the man over him into one of the heavy wooden tables, sending food flying.

Continuing the backwards roll to regain his feet, Jake ran forward, leapt into the air and planted a foot against the posterior of one of the brothers who was just regaining his feet. The force of the kick propelled him toward Jase and Jamie. Jase could not help slipping a leg in front of the brawler's fast moving feet, and was rewarded by the clunk of the man's head impacting a tree that stood slightly behind them.

The older brother regained his feet, and was met by three quick left jabs followed by a right to the midsection. As he bent forward from the blow, an elbow to the back took what was left of his wind and put him flat on the ground. The brother that had been thrown by the hip lock was back on his feet and connected a glancing blow to Jake's head. Catching the arm with his right hand, and buckling the man's knee with a foot placed behind the joint, Jake forced the arm up and back as he slammed his left hand to the back of the shoulder. With a dislocated arm, the last brother was out of the fight.

Brushing himself off, Jake donned the borrowed suit again, except the cussed bow tie that he placed in the pocket. Jamie, seeing his friend's discomfort, and being close to starting a scrap of his own over some of the comments, suggested Jake accompany him and Jase on some made-up chore, and meet the others later. When they had cleared the social, Jake thanked his friend for "getting him out of the worst fix he had ever been in" as he had not wanted to embarrass his niece. When Olga and her family arrived at home, she gave her uncle a kiss on the cheek, and promised to never again put him in such a situation. Having a better understanding of Jake and his needs, she realized the love her uncle had for her to allow himself to be put in a place where he felt so much discomfort.

A couple of days later, Jamie and Jase headed back to their home, and Jake to the far western mountains and deserts. The visit from his old friend had seemed to give Jamie more spirit and even more of a closeness to his son. Jase, also feeling this closeness, began working more often with his father at the forge, and was able to accomplish much of the basic work. Also, true to Jase's promise to himself, he and his father took time each day to work on fighting skills, along with Jase's schooling.

A few years later, Jase now a grown man could match his father's shooting skills and could usually best him throwing hawk and knife. However, though Jase had reached his full growth, the experience of the older man usually gave him the upper hand in their hand to hand combat. Jamie used skills varying from the boxing skills of the pugilist to the fighting arts of the Far East and, though Jase was learning fast, instincts honed by experience usually won out. Even when practicing knife fighting, done with sticks blackened in the forge so they would leave a mark when contact was made, Jamie's instincts usually brought him first blood.

For Jase's eighteenth birthday, Jamie surprised him with a knife he had made specifically for the occasion. The knife was rather plain looking, about nine inches long with a rawhide wrapped handle, but was built according to what Jamie felt Jase's needs might be. He had worked for over two years perfecting steel that would be strong yet flexible enough for throwing and still have the ability to be tempered to hold a sharp edge. Upon receiving the knife, Jase built a leather sheath to hold it firmly to his leg inside of his boot. Jase took great pride in his father's knife, which, as it would turnout, would be the only one Jamie ever made.

A week after Jase's birthday, Jamie left with a wagonload of his crafts to deliver in various towns around the area. Jase was unable to accompany Jamie on the weeklong trip because he was busy caring for the crops of a neighbor, who had injured his back. Jamie was about two days overdue when Jase spotted the wagon coming down the road driven by a man Jase knew only as Bob and accompanied by a sheriff and two deputies. Jamie's body was in the back covered by a blanket.

The sheriff related the story. He and a posse had been on the trail of a group of outlaws that had robbed a bank and killed two people. They had come upon the outlaws laying about the road a few miles back. Six of the seven were dead, with the seventh living just long enough to tell them what had happened.

The one telling the story had been shot during the robbery, and was having a hard time staying in the saddle. The group spotted the lone man with the wagon and decided to kill him and take the wagon to transport the wounded man. One of the outlaws shot the man as they rode up, but Jamie returned fire with his single shot weapons. Both rifle and pistol emptied a saddle, and he jumped from the wagon taking another rider to the ground with him. Fighting in close with his knife, so guns could not be used without fear of hitting one of their own, he killed all but the wounded man, who had fallen from the saddle when his horse bolted. After the fight, the man pulled himself into the wagon and started his horses down the road.

Leaving part of his posse to collect the bodies of the outlaws, the Sheriff and two deputies followed the wagon tracks, and those of three of the outlaw's horses that had followed the wagon. The wagon had followed the road for some distance before coming to a fork where the wagon had turned off. A short ways from this fork the trail came to a closed gate where the horses pulling the wagon stopped. The three outlaw's horses were there with the wagon, and the driver, Jamie, lay dead on the seat.

Asking around the area while trying to identify the man, they found Bob who knew Jamie and offered to accompany them to take the body home. Bob, the sheriff and deputies helped Jase lay his father to rest alongside Katrina on a hill behind the house and Jamie read passages from the Bible. As they left, Jase heard the sheriff utter the words he would always remember, and which would help guide him the rest of his life. With respect in his voice, the sheriff said "Jamie Richards, you were one hell of a fighter, you gave it your all and you never gave up." After the others left, Jase pondered a life he had never known, a life without his father.

CHAPTER 4

Realizing he lacked his father's ability to put out quality work and not wanting to soil the reputation his father had built, Jase shut down the forge except for his own use. He was able to supply most of his needs off the land, though game was getting scarcer as the human population grew. Needing little money to live, and having quite a sizeable amount that his father had saved up, he did not need to do outside work. He did, however, take odd jobs for others in order to stay busy. It was while working at one of those jobs that he had seen the girl.

He was repairing a porch for a well-to-do family when a girl, who had been visiting those at the house, tripped on a lose board and fell into his arms. In the brief moment he held her, before gently stabilizing her onto her feet, his heart fluttered and he broke out into a cold sweat. Jase stammered an apology for the loose board, at the same time as she was thanking him for saving her from a fall. He felt simultaneously embarrassed for his lack of words and elated by the music in her voice. He could not keep his mind on his work the rest of the day, and could see only her smile and wave as she rode away in her family's carriage. Little did he realize how much that chance meeting was to effect his life.

About four months later Jake showed up again. He said he had been in Nebraska Territory when he ran into a man who told him about a blacksmith that had wiped out a whole gang of outlaws single handedly. Of course by then, as the story was told, the number in the gang had grown to about twenty. Jake said he knew the blacksmith had to be Jamie, and upon hearing of his death started east the next day.

Jase ask Jake to stay until spring, and with winter coming on, Jake was glad to accept the offer. Though Jake's command of the spoken English language left something to be desired, Jase was surprised to learn that his reading skills were very good. Jamie had collected a few books, and Jake insisted Jase read some of them along with him. This reading helped to install a fondness for the written word in Jase. As he and Jake began spending time reading together, and discussing what they read, Jase found that besides knowing much about survival, and the ways of the wild country, the old man was well-versed on much of history.

During that winter, as they worked and

read together, Jase and the old man became very good friends. Jase also became friends with Olga and her family during the two trips they made to visit. Jake talked about times in the Nordic lands of the old country, and claimed his people were the first to visit these new lands, other than Jase's mother's people who were first here. Realizing he had said too much already, Jake stated only that through both his mother and father, Jase came from exceptionally good stock, and he should take care to never bring them to shame.

By the end of the winter, Jase had gained much in both knowledge and fighting skills through the time spent with the old man. He was sorry to see him go, and made Jake promise to write occasionally and to let him know where to send letters in return. Jake offered the opportunity for Jase to travel with him, but Jase declined, mostly because of his attachment to the place where he had been raised, but partially because of the girl.

Jase had only seen the girl one time since their first meeting on the porch. He was in town picking up supplies, when she came rolling by in their carriage. As she recognized him, a quick smile came on her face, and she sat straighter in the seat. He hesitantly raised his hand in a wave, and his becoming smile was automatic. She returned a pert wave and her face beamed. Jase's knees went weak, as his stomach tied into knots at the sight of her, but he was elated that she had recognized him. Encouraged by the brief encounter, he resolved to find out more about her.

He learned that her name was Priscilla Marsden, and that her family owned one of the plantations in the area. Her reputation was that of a prim and proper young lady, yet not full of the self-importance displayed by many of the well to do. Jase, having no idea of the expected behavior when courting a girl of society, decided to attempt to acquire work at the plantation in order to be around her and perhaps learn accepted social practice.

Unbeknown to either Priscilla or Jase, Priscilla's father Burleigh Marsden, or Burl as he was known, had noticed his daughter's interest in the young man and had made some inquiries of his own. Thus, by the time Jase made his decision, Burl already knew of his reputation as an honest, hard working man. Jase, being the son of a hard-working blacksmith with a reputation of taking pride in his work, did not come from a moneyed family like most of the others that had previously shown interest in Priscilla. However, Jase did seem to come from good stock, and family money meant little to Burl, who was the son of a ship's carpenter and had started with little money himself. Through hard work, and more than a little luck, Burl had built the plantation that supplied the life style they now enjoyed.

Burl was somewhat surprised though when Jase came looking for work. He had expected him to ask permission to call on his daughter, as was the common procedure in the society of the day. However, given an opportunity by the unexpected request, Burl decided to test both Jase's persistence and education. He told Jase that before he would consider employment, he would need a written list of Jase's skills and also the names of others for whom he had done work. Jase, already nervous and not actually expecting to be hired anyway, was about to dismiss the whole idea of working on the plantation when Priscilla entered the room.

Burl introduced his daughter to "Mr. Jason Richards, who may enter employment with us." Jase, not being used to such a formal introduction, and surprised by Priscilla's sudden entrance, turned red as he stuttered "H-H-How do you do, M-Miss Marsden?" "Please call me Priscilla" the girl answered, as she daintily offered her hand. Jase grasp her hand in his and like to shook her arm off before he remembered seeing a gentleman kiss the hand of a lady and realized his error. Excusing himself and almost running from the house, it was four days before he gained the courage to return with the well-written documents.

Burl was pleasantly surprised at the writing ability of this mountain boy and decided to test his abilities further. As Burl was showing Jase around the plantation to assess what work Jase might be able to handle, he asked Jase how many wagon loads it would take to transport the cotton crop to market. Jase requested the estimated yield and amount per wagonload before giving the proper answer almost immediately. As an afterthought, using the last price he had heard for cotton, he gave the estimated gross revenue. Burl found that not only could Jase read and write well, but he also possessed a good head for numbers.

A short time later, while they were discussing needed repairs on a wagon, Jase suggested an alteration to the plantation wagons that would increase the load they could transport. A quick estimate showed that with the modifications the number of loads needed to transport the expected crop could be cut by over ten percent. Burl and Jase discussed the modifications and they became

Jase's first job for the plantation.

Some metal work was required for the modifications, and though Jase had the equipment to make them, he doubted he had the ability to make them properly. With this in mind, he paid a visit to a blacksmith that had been a friend of his father. He had seen Brian Collins' work, which was a close match to Jamie's, and he was sure the man could handle the project, if he was willing to take on the job.

Brian was interested in the challenge presented by the modifications, but doubted that his small iron forge could handle the job. After discussing possible options, Brian and Jase made the trip to check the working limits of the larger brick forge Jamie had built. When Brian saw the forge, he stated he had seen none better, and was overwhelmed with the possibilities of work that might be turned out using it. Deciding the forge could easily handle the wagon pieces, the two men discussed the work to be done.

Brian had his normal amount of work to accomplish if he was to keep his customers, and each time he switched between the two locations it would cost him an extra day for the travel alone. This would severely limit the time he could spend modifying the wagons. Brian also mentioning that the owners of an emporium that borders the property on which his house and business are located were pressuring him to sell the property to them. Brian had mixed emotions over the offer as the business was in a good location and he had no reason to relocate. He feared however, that if he refused the emporium owners might use their connections within the local government to put him in a position where he would be forced to sell, possibly at a lesser price. Brian had been weighing his options and Jase gave him one more possibility.

Jase could see the appreciation with which Brian looked at his father's forge and felt he would care for it and use it wisely. He also knew that without use and care the forge would eventually fall to ruin. Weighing these things, he made Brian an offer of leasing the forge for a small percent of the profit. If the agreement worked out, Brian could buy part of Jase's land on which to build a house. For the time being, Brian could move his family into Jase's house and Jase would live in one of the outbuildings that made up the metal shop and barn. With the addition of Brian's smaller forge, and other equipment, the two men could work together on both Brian's orders and the converting of the wagons. Jase could do much of the rough work, and Brian would handle the finishing. Brian gladly accepted the offer and started home to make the sale of the property and prepare for the move.

Jase stayed to ready his place for their coming. He moved his personal things to a former storage room in the barn that he fixed up for his use. He then cleaned up the house. It was a sad chore as he thought back on good times spent there with his father. After he was satisfied that the place was in shape to accept Brian's family, he hitched up the wagon and headed down to help with the move.

It took over two weeks for the two men to get the shop into operation, but once they were started, things progressed better than planned. Jase and Brian worked well together and Brian's young son, Cameron, proved to be an exceptional helper. Adiella, Brian's wife, transformed the house into a thing of beauty and handibility as she made it into their home. Jase was pleasantly approving of the changes, and wondered how the house would have looked had his own mother lived. Adiella was also an excellent cook and Jase, being accepted as one of the family, ate well every time they sat down to the table.

The conversions of the wagons were done at the iron shop and Jase was only at the plantation when exchanging wagons. During these visits he would always stay long enough to spend some time talking with Priscilla, though he made no indication of his feelings for her. Their discussions were about the work on the wagons, other problems concerning the plantation, or general discussions of the day. Jase had at least learned to talk to her without the embarrassment and stuttering of the past. He had also found Priscilla to be knowledgeable about the management of the plantation and willing to pitch in when there was work to be done. He found her to be a strong, intelligent woman with the refinements of a lady.

Each enjoying the company of the other, they were fast becoming friends. Burl and his wife, Susannah, watched the friendship grow with approval, as both had come to like the man they saw in Jase. Burl began discussing more of the workings of the plantations with him and used many of Jase's ideas regarding everyday operations. He even offered Jase a small house on the plantation in which to live after the project with the wagons was finished if he would oversee part of the operations of the huge farm.

CHAPTER 5

One day, as he was working on the last wagon, Jase received word that Olga and her family had all been killed. A young girl from a neighboring farm had shown up at their door asking for help. Disheveled and crying, she stated that she had been raped by some men, and though she escaped, feared for her life. Olga sent Joe, a young man that had been helping them around the farm, for the law and began settling down the hysterical girl. Shortly after Joe left, five men rode into the yard looking for the girl. Sven, Olga's husband, ordered them off the place with a shotgun. However, when they turned as if to leave, two of the men shot him. Firing from a window, Olga wounded one of the men with her husband's rifle, but was herself shot in return. The men then stormed the house killing Olga's sons and the girl that they had previously raped. Quickly ransacking the place, they set it on fire and fled.

By the time Joe returned with the law, the fire had consumed most of the house with the three bodies inside. Olga and Sven were laying in the yard. A man and his wife had happened by shortly after the men left, and dragged Olga from the burning house. She related most of the story to the couple before succumbing to her wounds. Olga also stated that the leader of the group was a man named Roland Corbett. Corbett was well known around the area as a troublemaker and was suspected of other robberies and murders in the area.

Brian said that he and Cameron could finish the last wagon, which freed Jase to leave immediately for Olga's house. Taking an extra horse so he could switch off to give each a rest, he made the trip in less than two days. Arriving only a couple of hours before the funerals of Olga's family and the girl, Jase said his good-byes and some for Jake.

Olga, Sven, and the burned bodies of the boys were laid out in a row a short distance from the remains of the girl they had tried to help. Due to the circumstances of their deaths and because both families involved were well thought of, stores were closed and most of the community turned out for the funerals. This gave Jase a chance to gain more information about the circumstances of the deaths.

Besides the man Olga had shot, another had been hit by Sven's shotgun blast that he triggered off as he died. This man, along with another that had taken him to a doctor, were now in custody. They were seen forcing their way into the doctor's house and had been captured there. The man Olga shot had died before the outlaws left the yard and they took his body with them to avoid recognition. In order to preserve the identity of the group, the man's body was quickly buried in a shallow, unmarked grave in the hills. After capture, the wounded man led the authorities to the grave of the man who was identified as Henry Palmer, a man known to associate with Corbett.

The wounded man, who would only give his name as John Smith to protect his family, confirmed the ring leader as being Roland Corbett but knew the other man who was still with him only as Bull. The other man that was in custody refused to talk about himself, any others of the group, or the rape and killings. He was recognized by some that knew him as a man known only as Wallace and was believed to be a cousin of Roland Corbett. The Sheriff assured Jase that he had notified the surrounding communities that Bull and Corbett were wanted for questioning in the murders, and was quite sure they would be found. He also offered Jase the chance to observe any further questioning of the prisoners planned for after the funeral.

After the bodies were entered into the ground, Jase accompanied the Sheriff and a small group back to town for the questioning. Joe offered to stay on and care for Olga's place until Jake could be found and decide what to do with it. Jase accepted the offer on Jake's behalf, and intended to send wires and a letter informing Jake of all that had taken place after setting in on the questioning. He then intended to get a room at the hotel as he felt like he could sleep for a week after his long ride.

The group was met a short distance out of town by a dirty little man riding a bareback horse. The man was called Cloyed and a comment was made about him being the local drunk. He told the Sheriff he was sleeping behind some crates that were alongside a store located across from the jail, when he awoke to the sound of gunshots. Peering out from his hiding spot, he saw four men run from the jail and mount horses that were being held by another. The five men then rode out of town trailing a sixth horse. After he could no longer hear the horses, he entered the jail and found the deputy lying dead. Borrowing a horse, he then rode after the Sheriff

Uttering an oath, the Sheriff spurred his horse toward town with the others close behind. When they arrived, they found the deputy lying in a pool of blood. He had been shot three times, once through the head at close range. His pistol lay alongside his hand, but had not been fired. Entering the cell area, they found the wounded prisoner who was known as Smith still in his cell. His pants were soaked with urine and it appeared that he was on his knees when shot point blank in the head. An extra heavy load of powder had burnt part of his face away. Seemingly, the group had intended to break him and Wallace out but, after finding out he had talked, murdered him instead.

As other men came in from the funerals, the Sheriff formed a posse of fifteen men, including Jason, and started after the killers. They followed the outlaw's tracks until they came to a rocky area where the road split after crossing a stream. The posse of mostly inexperienced men milled around obliterating any sign that might have been left .by the outlaws. Frustrated, the Sheriff sent most of the posse back to town.

Nate Lawson, the brother of the slain deputy did not want to give up, so he and the Sheriff asked Jase to accompany them as they checked out a way-station some distance further on. They felt there was an off chance that the outlaws might stop there for supplies or food. The Sheriff led the way over a shorter, but seldom used, trail which brought them to the way-station just as the sun was dropping beyond the western horizon.

The route they had taken brought them into the yard from an angle that did not give them a full view of the front of the building, but the partial view they had showed no sign of any extra horses. The only sign of life was the soft light filtering from a window as a lantern was lit, and two men some distance down the road in a wagon. Deciding they had missed their quarry, the tired, hungry men's thoughts were on supper as they rounded the corner of the building.

The outlaws, having tethered their horses on the opposite side of the building due to a wagon blocking the front as it was being off-loaded, were just exiting the building. Wallace, recognizing the Sheriff, bellowed "law" as he fired his rifle from the hip. The quick shot went through the Sheriff's leg into his horse. Jase, who had been carrying his rifle over the pommel with the barrel facing away from the building, fired a hair slower than the outlaw. The Sheriff's horse was still falling when Wallace was slammed backward by Jase's bullet. His heart exploded, he collapsed to the porch and did not move again.

Nate and another of the outlaws fired at the same time. The outlaw missed, Nate's shotgun did not. Two other outlaws fired as they ducked back into the building. One bullet knocked the shotgun from Nate's hand, and the other showered splinters from a porch rail into Jase's face. After being knocked out of balance by the man Nate had shot, the other outlaw that was still on the porch was just bringing his rifle up for a shot when Jase fired his pistol. Taking a body hit, the man hesitated slightly then continued to bring the rifle level. Jase dove for the corner of the building as two rifles boomed almost as one. Powder burns on Jase's shirt gave evidence of how close the shot had come.

The other rifle shot had been that of the Sheriff as he fired over his dead horse killing the man on the porch. The rifle shots were followed by those of two pistols fired from inside the building. One hit the Sheriff's dead horse, and the other sang off the edge of the porch where Nate hugged the ground. As Jase reloaded his weapons, four more shots in rapid succession came from the revolvers of those in the building. They were aimed toward Nate and the Sheriff who were in the more precarious positions.

The men outside held their fire into the now darkened building for fear of hitting the proprietor or any other innocent persons that may be caught in the store. This gave the advantage to those in the store as they had no concern of others getting hurt and could fire anytime they found a target. Moreover, the Sheriff was pinned down behind his horse. Nate had been able to crawl along the edge of the porch to the corner where Jase was. However, he had to hold his pistol in his off hand as his shooting hand was numb from having the shotgun slammed from it.

As the moon rising above the trees began to replace the faded light of day, Jase left Nate to cover the door from the corner and began working his way around the building. He was trying to find a way to enter the building unnoticed, and checking to make sure that those inside were not trying to circle around behind them. He had just reached the back of the building when he heard a man ask the sheriff where his other two men were. ."Don't shoot," exclaimed the Sheriff, "He has a woman in front of him." Jase ran back to the corner of the building before giving his location.

Being assured that none of the men could get behind them, the two outlaws, using the proprietor and his wife as shields worked their way to their horses. Forcing the hostages to mount the horses with them, and threatening to kill them if shooting starts, they took off down the main road. As they left, Jase ran to help the Sheriff while Nate checked the outlaws on the porch and the inside of the store.

The store was empty and the outlaws were dead. The tough old Sheriff assured the men he would be all right and handing his weapons to the two men urged them to follow the outlaws and try to rescue the hostages. Jase handed the Sheriff an extra shirt to use for bandaging and the two men took out after the outlaws.

A short distance down the road the men came upon the proprietor trying to comfort his wife alongside the road. Once they were sure of no immediate pursuit, the outlaws threw the hostages from their running horses. Though scratched and bruised, the man was in good shape. His wife however did not fare as well as she suffered a broken leg and two broken fingers along with cuts and bruises and was in heavy pain. Making the lady as comfortable as possible and leaving Nate to watch over them, Jase went back to the way-station after a wagon and the Sheriff.

Jase and Nate took the Sheriff and the

others to a doctor in a neighboring town and then reported the incident to the authorities so they could collect the bodies of the outlaws. Jase then slept a few hours in an empty jail cell before he and Nate headed back. The Sheriff asked Nate to cover for him until he was back on his feet and Nate made sure warrants were issued on Corbett and Bull for the death of Nate's brother. Jase sent telegrams telling about Olga's family's deaths to three places that Jake was known to frequent along with sending a letter to the last address he had for Jake. He stayed for the funeral of Nate's brother before heading back to his own home.

Jase was well on his way and thinking about the events of the last few days when the realization that he had taken another man's life first entered his conscious thoughts. He was amazed that he felt no remorse. He had simply reacted to a situation that threatened others and himself. Wallace, through his disregard for others, had chosen the path that led to his violent death, and Jase could find no regret that fate had chosen him to be the implement of that death. He did however find himself reflecting on the probable sorrow of any family that the dead outlaw left behind.

As Jase contemplated the effects of the path the outlaw had taken, he began to think about the interactions of his own life. No matter what path a man chooses in this life he cannot help but effect the path of others. Even though one may feel he is alone on the path he chooses, he cannot help but alter his route according to those that have gone before and his passing will effect those that come after.

Even the most skilled woodsman cannot traverse a trail without leaving some evidence of his passing. As another finds that evidence, he will use a moment of his time to study it. Using past experiences gained as his path intermingled with the paths of others, he will decipher said evidence, which will then guide his own path. According to the decisions he makes, he may elect to continue along the path he is on, or may change his intended direction.

The influences that effect our paths begin at birth and end at death. However, the influences of our paths upon the paths of others will start before we enter this world and continue after we have left it. Jase realized that the knowledge they were to have a child was a major factor in Jamie and Katrina's decision to build a permanent home. Having a small child to care for was the major factor that kept Jamie tied to that home even after his wife's death. In fact, the decision Jamie made at that time eventually led to him making the trip on which he was killed. Jase realized that this influence of one's life on others was part of the outward flow represented by the flower-like stones of Jake's medallion.

Jase realized that the home his father had made for him had served the purpose Jamie had intended when he made the decision to settle there. It had provided a relatively safe place for Jase to learn as he grew to manhood. It gave Jase a solid place from which to start the many paths he would travel through life, as well as a haven to which he could always return, if only in his mind. Though gone, Jamie was never more present to his son as Jase made the decision to step out upon a path leading away from the home he had known.

CHAPTER 6

As Jase rode into the yard the finished wagon with a grinning boy setting in the seat was the first thing he saw. Cameron was fair busting with pride as Jase gave his approval of the wagon the boy and his father had finished together. Brian alluded that once the finished ironwork was done, Cameron had taken it upon himself to complete the rest of the alterations himself and had done them well. The men and boy then washed up for supper.

After the best meal Jase had eaten for some time, the men and boy sat on the porch and talked. Jase waited until Adiella and her daughter, Rose, joined them after the dishes were done before he stated what was on his mind. Rather than selling Brian part of the land on which to build, Jase offered them the house which had become more their home than his. He had decided to take Burl's offer and move to the small house on the plantation to pursue the things that were becoming his own dreams.

The family agreed to buy the house and property, but refused to negate their previous agreement regarding Jase having a percent of the profits from the forge. Brian insisted he would put Jase's share back so it would be available at any time Jase needed or wanted it. In addition, the family made sure Jase knew he would be welcome at any time, as he was part of their family even though he was not blood kin.

Using the last wagon that Cameron had finished, Jase moved his belongings to the small house on the plantation. Burl and Jase, who was now classed as an overseer, were almost as of one mind with all decisions being discussed between them. Burl concentrated his efforts on the general operations, while Jase took over the building and maintenance. Unlike most plantations, the women, Susanna and Pricilla, were included in the operations and often worked alongside of the men. They also handled the domestic decisions of their lives.

The natural attractions between Jase and Pricilla grew the more they were together and Jase ask for her hand in marriage in the coming spring. Jase, though never wholly comfortable at social gatherings, learned the ways of a proper southern gentleman and gave a good showing in the social world. With the exception of three or four would-be suitors of Pricilla, he was well liked by the social elite of the community. Never losing his connections with, and respect for, the working classes of people he was totally accepted among all those he dealt with no matter what his dealings with them.

Burl also never put himself above others even with the success of the plantation, nor did Susanna. They also raised their daughter with the same standards. As with most southerners, their slaves were treated as humans, rather than as possessions, and were very loyal to the family. Along with the ownership papers Burl held on each slave, he kept papers freeing them should something happen to him. This he did so that none could be sold into treatment he did not approve of. Jase observed one occasion where another plantation owner challenged Burl on his "coddling of his slaves." Burl refused to debate the issue. He simply turned his back and walked away leaving the man frustratingly talking to himself.

Due to the loyalty of his slaves, Burl was quite comfortable leaving the plantation to their operation. This gave him and his family the freedom to leave for extended periods without worry. One extended trip came after Jase received an answer to the letter he had sent Jake informing him about the loss of Olga and her family.

Jake was in Indian Territory where Jase

had sent the letter after being alerted to its existence by one of the telegrams Jase had sent to a supply point Jake used in Colorado. Being assured by Jase that Olga's family had been properly laid to rest, and that their killers were either dead or had left the area, Jake made the decision not to return. As next of kin, he sent papers authorizing Jase to take possession of Olga's and her family's belongings, to do with as he saw fit. Jake had heard that a renegade named Corbett was operating in Kansas and being quite sure the man was Olga's killer; Jake was headed there to try to track him down so that he might bring him to justice. Jase almost felt sorry for Corbett if the old man did find him.

As Jase made plans to make the trip to dispose of Olga and Sven's small homestead, Burl offered to accompany him. The women would also go along, as Jase wished Pricilla to meet both Nate and Joe. Jase had kept contact with both men and the three had become good friends. Taking the buggy, two saddle horses, and a wagon loaded with their supplies and driven by two of the slaves, they set out for a leisurely trip. Jase was pleasantly surprised to find that Pricilla had brought along some riding clothes, and they rode most of the trip together on the saddle horses.

Furthermore, both women settled in well to camp life and seemed to enjoy the break from the social restraints of the plantation.

When they arrived Jase found that Joe had built a small house on the foundation where Olga and Sven's once stood. As Jase had expected, the place was well cared for and in good shape along with what appeared to be a fine crop in the fields. They setup camp in the yard, and Joe offered the house for the lady's use, which they gratefully accepted. Jase and Joe then rode out to inspect the fields. While they were inspecting the fields, Jase could see the love Joe had for the place and the pride he took in it.

Joe, not knowing that Jase could do as he wished with the place, asked if Jase thought Jake might sell the farm, and what Jase felt he might want for it. He confided that he was courting a girl and though they had talked about marriage, and she was willing, he would not formerly ask her until he had a proper place to bring her. He had saved most of his wages and, although he knew it was not near enough, wondered if Jake might consider taking it as earnest money to hold the farm until he could save the rest.

As they neared the small rise where Olga's family and the girl were buried, Jase noticed a small, white picket fence surrounded by flowers. Joe said that Nate had helped him build the fence and Jasmine, the girl he was courting, planted and cared for the flowers. He and Jasmine worked together keeping the plot trimmed and looking nice. It was during this conversation that Jase decided what he felt Olga and Sven would want done with the place.

Back at the house, Jase asked Joe if he would ride over and invite Jasmine and her family for supper. Joe readily agreed, and as he left Jase asked him to let Nate know they were there and invite him also. After he had gone, Jase discussed his feelings about the farm with Pricilla, as he had taken to talking over matters of importance with her. Nate showed up shortly afterwards and, as he was a close friend of Joe's, Jase asked his opinion also.

After supper, Jase read Jake's letter to Joe and Jasmine's family. He told Joe that he would like him to take the place as a gift with two stipulations. The burial plot was to be kept up and Jake would always be welcome if he should wish to live there or visit. After the shock of the offer wore off, Joe asked Jasmine's father for her hand in marriage. Receiving her father's permission, Joe and

Jasmine accepted the offer together, and agreed to the stipulations. Joe even stated that he intended to put part of the money he had saved back, and it would always be available to Jake should he ever have the need.

While the others sat around listening to Joe and Jasmine make plans for their wedding and the farm, Jase and Nate wandered to the corrals and turned the horses out into the fenced pasture. Nate had taken over as deputy sheriff and he told Jase that according to the information they had received, Corbett had indeed been operating in Kansas. They had requested that the authorities there inform them if he was caught. They received word back that vigilantes had chased him out of the area and that he was believed to be hiding out somewhere in Nebraska Territory.

When the two men returned to the gathering, Burl, Jasmine's father, and her two brothers joined them. Conversation soon turned to the unrest between Washington and some of the southern states. The northern politicians had been forcing laws and tariffs on southerners, and there was talk about forming a southern government and separating from the union. Slavery was also an issue that came up at times even though many of the northern states were also slave-holding states. However, although there were many slave owners in the southern states, they were a relatively small proportion of all southerners. Of contention to most in the south was the idea of having their lives dictated by the more politically powerful northerners.

As a whole, the small group of men found, as they discussed the situation, that all were of a mind to rid themselves of the northern domination and try for a more equal government. Though war was a possibility, none felt it was likely and that separation would come peacefully. The Constitution gave any state the right to secede and, even though some in the north had shown little regard for the Constitution, it was doubted that the Union would go against it. However, should it come to a battle, all gave voice to doing what might be needed for the cause. The conversation soon broke up, and those not staying at the farm took advantage of a bright, moonlit night to head for their individual homes.

The next day, the men took care of the paperwork needed to deed the farm over to Joe, while the women were busy shopping. By the time the legalities were taken care of, and the women were dragged away from their shopping, the day was almost gone. Jase and

Burl decided to leave early in the morning and take a route that would take them by Jase's former house. As they left, they promised Joe that they would try to return the next month for the wedding. Three days later they pulled into Jase's old homestead.

Brian and his family were glad to see them and Cameron excitedly took Jase to see some of the metal work he was learning to do. The boy was turning into an exceptionally good blacksmith. When Jase commented about an addition being built to the back of the house, Brian grinned and said, "Were going to need it, we are expecting another young one in the spring."

After supper, Brian took a box from the mantle and slid it across the table to Jase. As Jase opened it, Brian said, "Business has been good, that is your share, partner." Jase slid the box back stating, "I'll collect when I need it, let it build." He then added, "That will be our emergency money, and you are welcome to use it if the need should arise, I don't need it right now." After spending the next day with Brian and his family, they returned to the plantation.

Jase was adding onto the small house at the plantation, so he and Pricilla would have it after they wed in the spring. The house was almost finished by the end of the year when word came that South Carolina seceded from the union. Seeing major change coming, Jase and Pricilla decided to be married the next month. Though not the gala affaire planned for the spring, the wedding was still the main social event at the start of the New Year. Nate made the trip to be the best man, and they were husband and wife a week before the confederacy was formed on February fourth.

Their love grew as their lives joined as one, and Jase was ever proud of the lady he had ask to share his life. She had shown herself to be strong willed and able during a trip to visit Brian and his family. While on the road, they were surprised by a sudden snowstorm and spent two days huddled in a makeshift shelter. Pricilla never uttered a complaint and handled the situation as though she had lived on the trail her whole life.

In April, about the time they had originally planned to be married, war broke out with the firing on Fort Sumpter. Jase felt compelled to join the war effort by enlisting in the army, but did so only after Pricilla agreed. Nate joined him, while Brian did his part by turning out iron works needed by the Confederacy. Burl put the plantation to growing supplies needed by the troops.

Nate and Jase joined the army at Camp McDonald in Big Shorty, Georgia. Due to Jase's expertise with weapons and Nate's experience as a deputy, both were given the rank of Sargent and assigned to training the green troops. Many of the soldiers, though most were hard working young men, had little experience with firearms. Some of the recruits brought their own weapons with them, as military weapons were in short supply, but few actually knew how to use them. Therefore, both Nate and Jase were kept busy teaching the care and use of a variety of shotguns, muskets, rifles, and pistols.

Pricilla and Jase moved into a small house just off the post so they could be together, and when Jase was at the post, Pricilla kept herself busy sewing uniforms needed by the troops. Nate bunked with the troops on the post, but often visited at the house. During these visits, the conversation usually turned to the training the troops were getting.

The soldiers were being trained as quickly as possible, which left many lacking of needed skills. However, the area most problematic to both Jase and Nate was the type of training. The men were being trained to attack in a broad, straight-line formation that left them totally vulnerable to enemy fire. Both men felt that the soldiers should be taught to make use of all available cover while working their way forward lessening their vulnerability to enemy fire. In their opinion, the type of warfare they were being taught dated back to the Roman Legions and would be suicidal when advancing toward the modern rifles and muskets of the northern troops. They knew that many of those they trained would die needlessly from the use of this outdated thinking.

Jase was granted leave over Christmas so he and Pricilla returned to the plantation for the holidays. They found that Burl had given his slaves their letters of freedom so that if anything would happen to him, they could not be sold into improper treatment. Though free to go, only three left the plantation after receiving their letters. The rest elected to stay on with the plantation and kept it running well.

Jase and Pricilla returned to Camp McDonald before the end of January and stayed through March. During the first part of April Jase accepted a request that he transfer as a sharpshooter to a Georgia unit he had trained the previous year. Leaving the weapons training to Nate, and a young corporal they had been grooming for the position, Jase took Pricilla home. He then continued north to join his new unit at Yorktown, Virginia.

Jase's unit was involved in almost steady fighting for the next four months. They fought battles at Yorktown, Richmond, Mechanicsville, Cold Harbor, and Malvern Hill. Jase's small squad of sharpshooters, while inflicting many casualties on the enemy, received few themselves. This was mostly due to Jase's insistence on using all possible cover while making every shot count.

During this time the mail moved reasonably well and Jase was able to keep reasonable contact with Pricilla and his friends. Most letters informed him that things were reasonably well at home, and he kept them informed of his movements as much as possible. With each letter he missed Pricilla more and knew she felt the same.

He received a letter from Pricilla in early August telling of some guerrilla activity in the area, but no major battles. All seemed well, but that was the last letter he received from her. Though he received a letter from Brian in late August, he felt the lack of a letter from Pricilla was due to his unit moving so fast that some of the mail could not catch up.

Just after the battle of Boonsboro,

another soldier from the area received a letter from home. He sadly gave it to Jase to read. The letter informed the soldier that his family was all right, but that guerilla actions were causing some problems in the area.

The letter stated that guerillas had hit the Marsden plantation, burning the buildings and killing some of the slaves that tried to protect the family and property. The other slaves were scattered and it was reported that the family was all killed. Jase thanked the soldier for sharing his letter, got up, and walked into the woods. There he allowed his emotions to take over. On his knees, he asked God "Why?" between loud sobs as he grieved for his beloved wife.

Jase, still not wanting to believe the news, wrote a letter to Pricilla telling her of his love for her. He then lost himself in the rigors of war. The Army of Virginia was moving onto Union soil, and moving fast. Jase seemed to handle his duties as usual, but his men noticed a change in his attitude. At Crampton's Gap, though he watched over his squad's safety, he was more aggressive with little regard for his own well being.

CHAPTER 7

At Antietam, his unit moved to reinforce other units that were being driven back over a hotly contested cornfield. Jase had just positioned his sharpshooters, when a line of soldiers that were charging to regain the already body littered cornfield began to falter. Jase ran among the smoke of the battle, rallying the men and charging forward with them. The shooting and cannon fire was so intense that little else could be heard, other than one's own thoughts. Jase and his comrades fought desperately to hold the ground they had gained only minutes before, but they were slowly being pushed back over a field littered with the bodies of men wearing both blue and gray.

Barely visible through the choking, thick smoke, Jase watched a solder he had just fired at go down. He was ramming another ball down the muzzle of his rifle as the blue line began another charge. Suddenly, he was knocked almost flat by the force of a rifle ball as it shattered his left arm. Partially in shock, he attempted to retrieve the rifle that had been knocked from his hand and found he could not make the arm work.

Kneeling on the ground, he set the cap on the rifle and raised it with his right arm only, forgetting to remove the ramrod. Pointing the rifle at one of two Union solders advancing on him from about twenty feet away, he fired. The feet of the solder left the ground as he was slammed backwards when both ramrod and ball shattered into his chest. Dropping the rifle, Jase reached for the tomahawk in his belt. Twisting his body, he felt a tug on his shirt as the other solders bayonet cut through it, just missing his side. The sharp edge of Jase's tomahawk cut into the arm of the solder, as he swung it while dodging the bayonet. As more solders folded in around him, some falling from the rifle fire of his comrades, he swung the tomahawk at one of them and missed. Bringing the tomahawk around with a back swing, he split the solders ear as the tomahawk sank into the side of his head. Suddenly, Jason's own head seemed to explode. There was a burst of bright light, and then all went black.

When consciousness came floating back, moving as though out of a mist, Jase was aware of tremendous pain in his left arm, and his head throbbed with every beat of his heart. As he lay there trying to gather his thoughts, he was aware of sporadic firing in the distance, shouting, and the cries of the wounded. As he raised his head to look around, he found the cold dead eyes of a Union solder staring back. The solder was partially sitting, leaning against two other piled bodies, one in blue and one in gray. The front of the solders blue coat was covered with blood and his lower jaw was missing, shot away by a rifle ball.

Still feeling as though he was only partially in this world, and having trouble holding his thoughts, he used his right arm to move himself into a seated position. With the movement, the pounding in his head intensified and he reached his hand up to find the source. The back of his head was wet and he could feel a split in the skin, evidently caused by the butt of a rifle. When he brought his hand back down, he could see the blood had started to congeal, which meant the wound had almost stopped bleeding. Although he was feeling very weak, his mind was starting to clear somewhat.

He checked his left arm, which would not move and was in extreme pain. Though his sleeve was soaked, there was very little blood seeping from the arm at this time. When he had fallen, his arm had become pressed between his side and the body of a dead solder, putting pressure on the wound. This pressure had stemmed the flow of blood allowing it to congeal enough to seal off the wound. His weakness told him he had lost a lot of blood, but landing on the dead solder had probably kept him from bleeding to death.

Though his ears had heard, his mind had not registered the sounds of people coming closer until a voice said, "Can you walk?" Jase looked up to see about a dozen Johnny Rebs being prodded along by three Union solders with rifles. All of the Rebs appeared to be wounded, though only a couple had to be helped along by others. Jase just stared and did not answer. He was not even sure he could get up. One of the Rebs, a big Sargent, said, "Come along lad and we will get you fixed up back there" as he nodded toward the enemy encampment. He and another comrade helped Jason from the ground and supported him, as he plodded weakly along with them.

By the time they reached the camp, the exertion had caused Jase's arm to begin bleeding heavily again and he was completely worn out. One of his comrades helped him pack and bandage his wounds, as the Union doctors were busy caring for their own men. Another Reb brought him some soup, that was mostly broth, and after he drank it, he slept until awakened by a doctor some time later.

After the doctor cleaned and checked the wounds, he began preparing to remove the arm. The rifle ball had shattered the bone, perhaps beyond repair, and there would be less chance of infection with a clean cut than with the jagged wound. Jase, however, refused to allow the arm to be taken off, preferring to chance infection and death. The doctor then agreed to try to repair the arm as best he could and started to work. He put the pieces of bone together as well as possible and manufactured a splint that would stabilize the arm yet allow care of the wound without the removal of the splint itself.

One of the Rebels was a man named Kendall who had some medical experience and had been assisting the Union doctors as they cared for all the wounded. He took it upon himself to help Jase care for the arm along with caring for the wounds of his other comrades. Because Kendall showed that his main concerns were with the wounded, rather than with the war, he was given more freedom to move about than the rest of the prisoners.

Having learned some of his healing skills while spending time with some friendly Indians, Kendall had learned to use some of the things readily found in nature for medicinal purposes. He used the added freedom to collect leaves, grasses and roots from the surrounding area that were usable for treatment of wounds and illness. At times, he would even find eatable plants to supplement the meager amount of food they were given.

At first, as the doctor had predicted, the wound on Jase's arm became infected and he became quite ill. However, as Kendall was able to find the roots and herbs he needed, the poultice he applied drew out the poison and the wound began to heal. Due to Kendall's care, Jase regained much of his lost strength and not being one prone to laying around, he began to assist around the camp. He and Kendall became good friends and, due to Jase's being labeled a cripple, and thus not likely to try to escape, he was allowed to accompany Kendall on his searches for roots and herbs.

The prisoners were moved along with the Union division as arrangements were being made to exchange them for Union prisoners held by the Confederacy. This constant changing of locations allowed Kendall to find enough roots and herbs to keep a sufficient supply. As Jase and Kendall were searching for herbs during one of the stops, Jase happened upon a small axe apparently discarded by troops that had previously bivouacked in the area. The handle was broken off, so Jase strapped the head to his body under his clothing where it could not be seen. This could make a useful tool or weapon, if needed. He had no fear of discovery, as the prisoners were never searched. In fact, he still had the knife his pa had given him tucked in his boot. He had eluded the original search that was done after their capture because he was in such bad shape he had not been expected to live.

By the time the prisoners were to be moved to the exchange point, their ranks had grown to about forty men. Most had been transferred from other units, but a few were new captives. The prisoners were informed that according to the Dix-Hill Cartel, that regulated the exchanges, they would be required to sign a paper promising to never again take up arms against the Union. When it became Jase's turn, he refused to sign the oath. He stated that he would not make a promise he may not be able to keep. Kendall, on the other hand, realized he could still serve the cause by working with the wounded and accepted the terms of the exchange.

Before Jason and five others that had

refused to sign were moved to a different area where they could be kept under heavy guard, he and Kendall had time to say goodbye. Kendall gave him some of the supply of herbs and instructions on care of his wounds along with those of another solder in the group. Shortly after the six dissenters were taken away, the rest of the prisoners were started toward the area of exchange.

The six dissenters were taken to a holding area where they joined a larger group of Confederate prisoners being transferred to the permanent prison facility at Camp Chase, Ohio. Taken by train to Columbus, they were then marched to the prison stockade. There they were divided into groups and assigned to wood-framed huts or barracks. The buildings were far from tight, so they blocked little cold, and the whole camp was infested by rats. Food was in short supply and clothing very limited. Most of the prisoners were in poor shape, with many being sick and dying.

Jase was able to keep himself in reasonable shape by finding ways to constantly work his body. He had even gotten some use of his arm back but was careful not to show the gain around others. Being regarded as a cripple, he was not as closely watched as many of the others. So with less observation, he was able to achieve time to work in solitude. Using this time alone, he had made a short handle for the axe head he had found and incorporated it into the arm splint. With the handle protruding down the arm as part of the splint, the head, being strapped to his shoulder, remained hidden. This also helped limit the use of the arm, which was what he wanted when not working to regain usage of it. The bone was knitting well, though somewhat crooked, and the torn flesh was healed over by early winter

Jase had never accepted being a prisoner of war, but had not felt too oppressed by it while traveling with the unit that had captured him. However, from the time he had entered the stockade he had struggled with the feelings that being closed in caused. Raised away from towns free to roam as he pleased, being caged in one place was exceptionally hard on him.

Though he was friendly and helpful to those imprisoned with him, he avoided close relationships with others. He wished to be responsible for no one but himself and friendships add responsibilities. He intended to find a way to escape this confining place and did not want to involve others. He was always aware of even small things that might help to make an escape possible.

He made some plans and felt he had found some possibilities of escaping the compound. One problem that he faced was his lack of knowledge about what lay outside of the compound. He would be easily recognized as a confederate prisoner and did not know where he would go once out of the fence. He needed more information than what he had observed coming in and what he could glean from others that had been outside for one reason or another.

On one cold day in February, the ground was solid mud left by the previous few days of rain and snow. The men in Jase's group were huddled around the small stove in their hut trying to stay warm when they were ordered to fall out. Grumbling, they moved from their shelter to the muddy yard where they were made to stand under rainy, overcast skies.

Mud slick roads were making travel almost impossible, and a small unit assigned to transport some wagons and large guns were bogged down not far from the prison. Prisoners were offered extra food and blankets to any willing to help free the equipment. Most of the prisoners would not leave the limited shelter of the buildings. For others however, the promise of added food and blankets was enticement enough for them to bear the cold.

Jase was one of the first to volunteer as it would give him a chance to observe more of the area outside the compound. Almost turned down due to his being a cripple, he convinced the guards that two good legs and one good shoulder were all that was needed for the job at hand, and was allowed to go. When the prisoners, about twenty five in all, and their guards reached the location they found a worse situation than they had been led to believe. The road ran along side of a swollen creek and one wagon had already been lost as it had slid into the raging water. Another wagon and one of the guns hung dangerously over the edge. Some of the prisoners were ordered into the edge of the creek to push on the wagon from that angle.

After a short struggle, the wagon was again on the road. Attention was then turned to the gun, with that problem attacked in the same manner. Jase was under the cannon lifting from the edge of the creek when the hitch snapped. Rolling off the bank, the big gun went into the swirling water, taking five of the prisoners with it.

Jase struggled in the freezing water for what seemed an eternity before he was able to catch hold of a root protruding from the bank and pull himself free from the raging torrent. He lay on the bank a few minutes, gasping for air, and then took notice of where he was. He had made it out on the opposite bank, some distance downstream from the wagons. Not being able to see the wagons or guards, he began walking away from the stream. The accident had almost cost him his life, but had given him a chance at freedom. He doubted they would even look for him, presuming him drowned. However, he was wet, cold, and had scant clothing. If he did not find shelter quickly, freedom would turn into death as he succumbed to the cold.

Walking fast, as much to keep his body manufacturing heat as to cover ground, Jase traveled in a direction that took him away from both the prison and the creek. Finding a small building that was mostly fallen to ruin, he crawled into a hole that led under a section of fallen roof. Shaking so hard that it was a struggled to unbutton his light jacket and ragged shirt, he stripped off his half-frozen clothing and slumped to the earth floor.

As his eyes adjusted to the darkness of the shelter, he searched the ruin for discarded clothes or anything else to use for cover. Finding nothing in the area, he searched through a couple of rat nests to see if they had used any cloth in their making that might indicate something of use in another part of the building. The nests yielded only twigs and dry grass, but would make good tinder for a fire if he could find some way to light it.

Remembering a pile of rock chips, evidently the discard of some type of stone working, he tested several types for spark by striking them against his axe. Finding one that would indeed produce spark, he took it to where he had the rat nests piled on the floor. It took several tries before a spark produced smoke from the nest material. Blowing lightly on the source of the smoke, he finally had a small fire. He was going to live.

Chopping off pieces of the driest wood he could find on the crumpled building, he kept the fire small and with little smoke. Any smoke that escaped from the structure could not be easily seen against the gray sky. Much of the smoke stayed in the enclosed area, but it was of little bother when weighed against the life-saving heat. As his clothes dried, he slept naked on the floor next to the fire. Even naked, he was warmer than he had been in days.

Not wanting to leave the warmth of his shelter, he had to force himself out into the cold of early dawn. In case a search was ordered, he wanted to put as much distance between himself and the prison as possible. Having reworked the splint to give some support to the arm, while still allowing movement, he carried the axe on his waist.

The sun shown brightly and warmed the day to a bearable temperature as he walked along. Even the saturated ground began to dry which made walking easier. Walking steadily, he stayed on little used trails, avoiding main roads as much as possible. By late afternoon, he had found some of the eatable roots Kendall had taught him to look for so, though still hungry, he had some nourishment during the day.

About an hour before sundown, he spotted a small farm in a valley. The main road looped around it as it progressed off the hill and through the valley. A shorter, more difficult, route went down a steep water shed, through the farmyard, and back to the main road. The water shed showed no usage since the storm, so Jason decided to wait there for darkness.

Having been cold all day and getting colder, Jason decided to slip into the farm to try to find a coat or blanket and perhaps some food. He was not one to steal and would much rather have asked for help than take what belonged to others. However, in his present situation, he had to avoid people and needing food and clothing to survive, was left with no alternative.

Finding a hollowed out place in the bank that would supply a bit of protection from the cold while he waited, he was busy using the axe to dig it deeper when he heard a running horse. Jase stood there, frozen, as the horse left the main road onto the trail. As the blue coated rider saw Jase, he reined in the horse and his hand reached for the pistol on his side. Jase, reacting in self-defense, stepped into the throw as the axe left his hand. The solder had just lifted the flap of his holster, when the force of the axe splitting his breastbone knocked him off his horse. Jase slid the knife from his boot and was beside the solder almost before he hit the ground. The knife was not needed. The solder's eyes closed as he drew his last gurgling breath.

Jase removed the gun belt and pulled the coat from the body of the dead solder before the blood from the wound could stain it. The solders heavy shirt was already soaked with blood so Jason did not remove it. Sliding into the warm coat, he talked softly to the black horse as he walked slowly towards it. The horse shied slightly, but stood still, nuzzling

Jason's face as he stroked the horses' neck. Having the black calmed, he tied the reins to a bush and returned to the dead solder.

After buckling the pistol belt around his own waist, he removed the solders boots and pants. Pulling the axe free from the body, he wiped it off with the solder's shirt. Had he not done this, he would have missed the cloth pouch strapped under the shirt. Removing the pouch, he stuffed it in a pocket of the coat then dragged the body to the hollow of the bank. Folding the body into the hollow, he caved the bank down to cover it so it would not be easily found. Tying the boots and pants to the duffel behind the saddle, he mounted the horse and headed west down the main road. He wished to use what little daylight was left to gain some distance from the area before making camp for the night.

CHAPTER 8

As the last light faded from the sky, Jase dismounted by a stream a short distance off the road. The place chosen was a grassy area where the stream ran through a fold in the hills in which higher ground blocked any view from the road. Removing the saddle and other gear from the horse, Jase picketed him close to the stream, yet where the Black could also reach the place where Jase intended to bed down. Through a soft voice and gentle touch during their short ride, a bond was already forming between horse and man and the Black showed a desire to be close to Jase.

In the dim light supplied by the sliver of a moon and the stars, Jase started to examine the belongings he had acquired from the dead soldier. First making sure the newly acquired pistol, a Colt revolver was loaded and capped, he then picked up the bedroll from the top of the pile. Having initially intended to examine the rifle in the scabbard that was next on the pile, exhaustion and the warmth and comfort suggested by the bedroll took precedent. Spreading the bedroll, he patted the Black's neck and slid into the promised warmth of the best sleeping accommodations he had in months. He started to think about the events of the day, but as his eyes closed so did his mind and sleep came easy.

Jase awoke refreshed with first light, and the first sensation he felt was that of hunger. The second was one of peace and safety, though he knew that in reality this might be an illusion. Rummaging through the gear, he found some coffee, a tin cup, a type of dried biscuit and some jerky. Checking the direction of the slight breeze to make sure the smell of smoke would not drift toward the road, Jase made a small fire of dry wood using matches he found in an oiled pouch. Putting coffee grounds in the cup and setting it at the edge of the fire to heat, he picked up the scabbard he had laid aside while looking for food. Sliding the rifle free, he was surprised to find it one of the newest Henry repeaters. It was carrying a full load, and he found over one hundred rounds of ammunition in one of the saddlebags along with extra bullets and powder for the Colt.

Dribbling cold water into the steaming cup of coffee to settle the grounds, he took a sip of the first coffee he had tasted for a long time. Dipping the hard biscuit in the coffee to soften it as he ate it and the jerky, the coffee was soon gone and he added more water to the grounds and again set the cup next to the fire. While this was heating, he further inspected his newly acquired belongings.

He found two shirts, one of them wool, and an extra pair of trousers along with a light jacket. The well-made boots he had taken off the soldier were in good condition and, though not perfect, were a reasonable fit when worn over one of the three pairs of stockings that were rolled up with the shirts. Other miscellaneous items for personal comfort, including a scarf and a pair of leather gloves, were also among the belongings. Wrapped in an oilskin pouch in the bottom of one saddlebag, Jase found a small bundle of letters. Settling the grounds in the cup, Jase sipped the coffee as he read them.

Though not fond of prying into the man's personal life, Jase wished to know more about him as the belongings he left behind seemed more and better than those of the average soldier. From the letters, Jase surmised the soldier belonged to a well-to-do family in New York. To insure their son was properly outfitted for his volunteered service to "This Great Union," the parents had bought him the best of clothing, weapons, and even the Black horse. The only thing that seemed to be actual army issue was his hat. Even the heavy coat Jase now wore was tailored for their son to meet military specifications. Influence was even used to have the young man assigned as a dispatch rider in a relatively safe area of the war.

In an unfinished letter found with the rest, the young man had asked his father to rescind his request for the safe assignment and allow him to join a Calvary unit at the front lines of the battle. He stated he "Was complying with his duties to the best of his abilities and doing his best to make them proud." However, "He had joined to fight Rebs, and was not being allowed to venture where the fighting is." The last entry said that he was carrying a dispatch to the front and would perhaps see some action there.

At mention of the dispatch, Jase remembered the pouches built onto the front of the saddle. In the first, he found an expanding telescope, but no papers. In the other, he found the sealed dispatch. Removing the seal, he read the orders for an attack against southern units. His first thoughts were to ride to warn the endangered Confederates, but quickly realized there was no way he could relay the information in time to make a difference. He would have to be content with the knowledge that his blocking the dispatch might disrupt the Union plan and stop, or at least delay, the attack.

Washing himself in the cold stream, Jase donned the captured clothing. To all outward appearances, he was a Union soldier. Inwardly, he was a man whose future had been taken away and whose drive for life had been worn thin by the rigors of battle. To him, all that remained was his seeming inbred drive for survival and a desire to examine the Far West that had been so dear to his father and Jake.

The Black playfully nudged Jase as he doused the fire and sorted the gear for loading, but stood quietly as he accepted the saddle. After filling the canteen that was with the horse, Jase road carefully to the road and started his trek west. Via information that had filtered down to the prisoners at Camp Chase, he knew about some of the problems that happened the previous year with the Sioux Indians in Minnesota. He decided to try to convince others he encountered that he was a Union soldier headed to assignment with troops there and felt he could make his disguise believable.

He would need to buy some supplies with a few coins he had found in the dead soldier's trouser pockets and felt the encounter with others would be a good test of his illusion. He also hoped to pickup more knowledge about situations toward his destination as the stores and saloons in the various settlements were often the best clearing houses for information. Much could be learned by simply directing the conversation to a subject and the mental filtering of the results. Seeing a town in the distance, he urged the Black into a lope, being anxious to test his disguise.

Should things go awry, Jase checked his weapons before entering the town. He then rode purposefully among the scattering of buildings to one that displayed a sign reading "General Mercantile". Hitching the Black with a slipknot, in the event he would have to move fast, he entered the establishment. The building was occupied by a slim man standing behind the counter, two women discussing some bolts of cloth, and three men playing cards on a cracker barrel in front of the potbellied stove that stood in the middle of the store. The three men looked up as the door opened and two of them nodded at Jase before returning to their cards. The women, both young, pretended to continue looking at the cloth, but their quiet conversation changed to a discussion about the rugged looking young soldier.

The man behind the counter moved to wait on Jase. "Can I help you corporal" the man asked with a smile. "Just need to replenish my grub supply" Jase answered, "got a ways to go yet". "Where you headed, if you can say" the clerk asked as he pointed out the various food goods on display. "Minnesota, I'll take some of that bacon and some flour" Jase answered. "Heard they are building up troops out that way to chase those stinking Indians out of the country" came a comment from the area of the stove. It was the man who had not acknowledged Jase when he first came in.

Another man at the stove added, "A detachment of soldiers came through t'other day n said they were planning a big push come summer." "Seems odd you traveling through alone" he continued in a questioning tone? "Liable to be some more through this way" Jase said, "they're hand picking some of us for a special unit." "What fer?" asked the first man. "Won't know till I get there" Jase answered, "Just got orders to report to Fort Ridgley for special assignment." The third card player, a sour looking man, spoke up, "Figures, they take our best men away from fighting them damn Rebs and send them out chasing stinking Indians." "You got a point Moe" stated the first man, "They ought to send them black

Niggers that all this fuss is about out to fight them damn injuns. Maybe they would kill each other off and us whites could get on with living" he added. Though there was much he would have liked to have said, Jase held his tongue as the two racists continued their discussion, having turned their attention away from him.

Jase used most of the money to pay for the food he had picked out, and was starting to leave, when the second man spoke up again. "Looks like you already seen some rough times" he commented as he mimicked the odd movements of Jase's twisted arm. "I fared better than a lot of lads" Jase answered, as he tipped his hat to the women and headed out the door. "God be with you son" the man said as the door was closing. Jase stored the food in his saddlebags, and returned the wave of two boys as he headed out of the town. As one of the card players' watched Jase leave, he stated "Judging by his accent, I bet he was one of them Kentucky boys that came up to fight the Johnny Rebs." "Probably so" commented another, "deal."

Having been able to purchase only enough supplies to last for two or three days, Jase set to thinking about finding some way to supplement the few coins he had left. He had thought about inquiring about possible work that might be available, but with his disguise as a soldier, this might raise suspicion. The few belongings he had acquired from the dead soldier were mostly needed and left little that might be traded. He was going over these acquirements in his mind when he remembered the belt pouch he had taken from under the dead man's shirt. Stopping by a stream, so both he and the horse could drink, he removed the pouch from the coat pocket. Opening the pouch, he was surprised so see it contained bills of U.S. currency and some gold coins. He did not count it at this time, but knew it was more than an average soldier would ever see. Taking a couple of the bills and stuffing them into his pocket, he strapped the pouch around his own waist for safekeeping.

Content that he no longer had to concern himself with acquiring money, he began to think about longer-range plans. The ruse of being a union soldier had worked well at the last stop, but Jase did not like being taken for a person he still considered as the enemy. Besides, there was always the chance he might run into someone who knew the dead soldier and recognize his horse and gear. Oft times people will recognize something, or someone, in the context they know them from, yet not in another. The horse carried no brand, but had some spattering of gray and white that were somewhat distinctive. The saddle, though well built, was not distinctively different other than the built in pouches, which were not a common thing. So it was unlikely either would be recognized on their own, but with a soldier aboard, an acquaintance of the dead soldier's might take a closer look.

Weighing the situation, Jase stopped at a small general store that seemed to service the many small farms in the area, as well as being an eating place for travelers along the road. He bought a brown, medium weight, coat that was long enough to cover the heavy military one he wore. He also took the proprietors suggestion of a bowl of beef stew and cold glass of milk. Short of the meals Adiella had prepared when he was last at the homestead, Jase allowed this to be the best meal he had eaten since and ordered another round of both the stew and the milk.

That evening Jase, as had become his custom, camped in a secluded area some distance from the road. Building his usual small fire, he cooked potatoes, bacon and three eggs he had carried carefully wrapped from the general store. He had bought a small pan and skillet at the store and though they took more room in his duffel, supper cooking in the skillet and coffee boiling in the pan made it seem that they were well worth the extra bulk.

While he ate, he removed the braid from the military hat and soaked the hat in the stream. Using an assortment of rocks to hold the position until it dried, he reshaped both the crown and brim so it no longer resembled the military style. Deciding that any altering of the military coat would be too visible, he elected not to try to change it. The overcoat he bought would cover it on cold days, and it could be carried out of sight in his duffel on warmer ones. Trimming the braid with his knife, and soaking it in a boiling mixture of dried berries, leaves and flower peddles, it was soon in no way similar to the gold band it had been before.

With nothing visible that could connect him with the military, Jase became a farmer who had lost everything when his place was destroyed as the war raged around it. Hoping to start over, he was looking for land further west. He even spent a few days traveling with six wagons belonging to a group of people that were moving westward away from a war they never wanted. Using the excuse of having to find work in order to continue, Jase left the wagons after they ferried across the Mississippi River and angled north toward

Minnesota. In actuality, Jase had decided to buy some trade goods with the money from the pouch and try to build some profit by trading.

Jase had also borrowed a pen and ink from one of his fellow travelers along with some writing paper. Before he left them, he had finished a letter to the dead soldier's parents. He informed them that their son had died bravely in the line of duty. He regretted that there was need to bury the body in an unmarked grave, but assured them that it was a single place and not a mass trench. Adding that he was sorry for their loss, he signed it "Sincerely, another soldier." Sealing it with tree pitch, he gave it, along with money for postage, to one of the men with the wagons to mail at the next postal stop they found. In this way, Jase felt the family would at least not wonder if their boy was coming home.

CHAPTER 9

About two days after Jase left the wagons, he was traveling along a seldom-used road and came upon an overturned wagon when he heard a weak call for help. Circling to the far side, he found a man lying with both legs pinned under the heavy wagon. Jase tried to lift the wagon to free the man, but it proved too heavy to lift by hand. Taking down a section of rail fence, he forced the rail under the wagon close to the man's legs. By rolling a rock under the pole to use as a fulcrum, he was able to lift the wagon enough for the man to drag himself free. One of the man's legs was broken but the other, though heavily bruised, was still usable.

Jase used strips of cloth torn from his old shirt and some branches to make a splint to stabilize the broken leg as the man explained his predicament. Sometimes hesitating as he gritted his teeth against the pain, the man gave his name as Tom Cromwell. He said he had a farm some distance up the road and was returning home from delivering a hog he had butchered and sold, when a raccoon ran under his horses causing them to spook off the road. As the wagon overturned, it knocked one of the horses down before the tongue snapped freeing the horses to run away dragging the piece of tongue between them.

Seeming to sense the need, the Black stood perfectly still as Jase struggled to get the wounded man in the saddle. Although in great pain, Tom never complained as they headed up the road with Jase leading the Black. They had gone about two miles when Tom's wife, Mary Jane, and their son George met them. When the horses had shown up without Tom and dragging the part of the tongue, they had hitched two of their other horses to their smaller wagon and come looking for him. Switching Tom to the wagon for easier travel, the group continued to the farm.

When they arrived, Tom's injuries were assessed and Jase offered to help transport Tom to a doctor to have the leg set properly. However, the closest doctor was in a larger town some distance off and Tom did not feel he could make the trip. Though the twist of the leg showed a bad break, no sharp bone had penetrated the skin. Having broken bones before, Tom felt a doctor could do no better setting it than those present, so he asked Jase if he would try to set it and perhaps eliminate the long trip to town. Jase agreed to try and began preparations.

Using wooden slats and leather strapping, Jase and George built a splint to use once the leg was set. Then, with George helping stabilize Tom, Jase and Mary Jane pulled and twisted the leg as Tom, biting on a strip of leather gave only a slight grunt of pain as the leg grated into place. When the splint was applied, only slight adjustment was needed for it to hold the leg solidly immobile.

After ascertaining that Jase had no pressing business, Tom made an offer to hire him to help around the farm until the family could handle the work on their own. Jase agreed to stay on and help, but refused to agree to the offer of pay, stating they would discuss it later. He knew only that the family needed the help, but knew nothing of their finances so refused to lock them into any agreement. While Tom rested and Mary Jane began preparing supper, Jase and George went out to care for the horses. Due to Tom's pressing needs, though the horses had been unhitched and turned into the corral, they still wore their harnesses and the Black his saddle. Just as the two finished checking the horses for possible injury and rubbing them down, they heard the call for supper.

Mary Jane set a good table, though in Jase's opinion she was not quite the equal of

Adiella, and while they ate, they discussed the needed work. Preparation for planting was just getting started and some care of their small amount of animals would be needed along with some repairs around the place. Of first concern though was the righting and repair of the wrecked wagon, but that would have to wait until morning. After supper, Jase was given a comfortable upstairs room in the two-story house and moved his gear into it. Working together, he and George finished the chores and they all retired for a much needed rest. Smiling at Tom's barely audible snoring that came drifting up the stairs, Jase soon joined the chorus as he settled into the well-made bed.

After breakfast the next morning, Jase and George left with the smaller wagon taking rope, block and tackle to right the overturned wagon. They also took tools to repair the fence Jase had torn apart to use while releasing Tom. When they reached the wreck, they took more of the long poles from the fence. They lashed these together to form a tripod that they then stabilized by tying it to the other wagon. Hanging the block and tackle from the tripod, and using the horses for power, they soon had the wreck back on its wheels. Finding no other major damage, they lashed what was left of the tongue to the back of the other wagon and repaired the borrowed fence. The project went well and they were back at the farm in time for a late lunch.

Over the next month or so, Jase and George worked together to repair the wagon and prepare the fields for planting. George, who was five years younger than Jase, proved to be a strong, able and willing worker. He also had a quick mind and learned new things easily. They each took an instant liking to the other and working together helped solidify their friendship. Jase soon found himself sharing much of the knowledge and skills he had learned from Jake and his father with the young man. By working with George, Jase also found that the teaching of these skills had honed his own almost to the point where they had been before he was shot. With the exception of the limits imposed by his wounded arm.

Tom had healed enough that by using a crutch he had made, he was able to help with most of the work. Though weather dictated another couple of weeks before planting could actually be done, the fields were ready and the farm and animals were in good shape. With little else needing done, and Tom's assurance they could handle the planting without him,

Jase decided it was time to continue on his way.

When Tom tried to pay Jase out of their meager funds, Jase refused. He stated that the room and board along with an old sheep skin coat Tom had given him to wear, were pay enough. He even offered to buy one of their horses and an old packsaddle. The packsaddle was one that had not seen use for some time and the horse was a well-trained sorrel Jase had become fond of as he used him around the farm. The family, though wanting him to take the horse and saddle as pay, finally accepted a fair price for them. They did however insist that he accept a few small items they were not using, but that Jase had need for.

The next morning after the deals were made Jase was packed and ready to leave before they all set down to breakfast. After the meal, Tom made the statement that Jase had shown himself to be a true friend. He added that one true friend could not refuse a gift from another, as he held out a Le Mat revolver toward Jase. Tom had taken it as trade for some goods a few months back and had noticed the interest shown by Jase when he first saw it. Though Jase would have gladly paid dearly for such a fine weapon, common courtesy dictated that he accept the pistol when offered. George then handed him the forty-two caliber mold that went with it and a sack of balls he had already formed. These were a necessity with the pistol, as the forty-two caliber was uncommon and readymade ammunition was hard to come by.

As they all shook hands, Tom gave Jase the name of a trader he knew to be honest along with a letter of introduction to insure fair dealing. The trader was a few days further along Jase's intended route and was reputed to have a large supply of goods. When Jase found the trader, he proved to be as honest as Tom had promised and by the time Jase had finished dealing he had spent over half the money in the belt pouch. He left the man's establishment with a second pack horse and a good supply of trading goods that he felt he could turn at a good profit. He also bought a supply of lead, caps, and powder for his weapons, along with a well-made tomahawk to replace the one he left on the battlefield.

Jase slowly worked his way to Fort Ridgley and the Sioux reservations in Minnesota. Trading with settlers and fellow travelers along the way, he had built a reputation as a fair and honest trader that preceded him to the fort. This reputation helped him acquire government permission to trade on the reservations, but did not set well with less scrupulous traders already established in the area. Many of these traders were far from fair and honest when dealing with the Indians, cheating them whenever possible. These treatments, along with failed promises by the government, were the main causes of the uprising the year before.

As Jase sat down to a meal of steak and eggs in the saloon, one of these traders began to voice his opinion. He spoke loudly about outsiders coming in and stirring up the Indians by the way they treat them. He talked about how they could start another uprising by raising the savage's expectations of how they should be treated and cause other problems. Though his talk was pointedly aimed toward Jase, he addressed his talk to others in the room until Jase was almost finished eating.

As Jase's sharp knife cut through the last piece of steak, the trader turned directly at him. The trader, bolstered by more than a couple of glasses of whisky, challenged Jase's honest trading with regards to the Indians. Not looking directly at the man, Jase forked the last piece of steak into his mouth before he spoke. "I was taught that a real man deals honestly with everyone" Jase stated as he savored the last piece of meat. He added, "So, unlike you, that is what I do."

The contrast of Jase's quiet, unconcerned voice compared to the loud, menacing one of the trader brought the room to silence. The trader stood glaring at Jase a few seconds as the words sunk in. He then screamed "I'll show you a real man," as he reached for the gun at his side. Jase rose slightly off his chair with a half turn toward the man as the knife flew from his hand.

The Trader's pistol had not cleared leather when the knife nicked his breastbone as it buried into the hollow at the base of his neck. His knees folded under him, blood sprayed from his mouth as his breath left him and his dimming eyes stared in disbelief at Jase. Before his body reached the floor, Jase was standing with feet spread, a pistol in each hand and eyes covering the whole room.

As the shock of the quick action left the room, three men bolted out the door. Two others moved to check the fallen man and the others, holding their hands out in a way that showed submission to the threat of Jase's guns, held their places. Jase, perceiving no further aggression, holstered the colt. With the Le Mat held in his left hand, he stepped forward and pulled his knife from the lifeless body. Returning to his table, he laid the pistol within easy reach and began wiping the knife clean. He had just returned the knife to the sheath in his boot, when one of the men returned with the Sergeant of the Guard and three troopers.

Though the troopers stood with rifles at ready, no attempt was made to disarm Jase, or otherwise harass him as the Sargent talked to witnesses. The Captain of the Guard and the post surgeon came in just as the Sergeant was finishing his investigation. The surgeon checked the body and, after taking the Sergeant's report, the Captain ordered the troopers to remove the body. He then came and sat down at Jase's table.

He ask Jase his opinion of the incident, and Jase answered simply, "As you already know, he was spoiling for trouble and left little option when he drew on me." He added, "I just did what I had to in order to survive." "That is the way I see it also" answered the Captain as he offered his hand, "You are free to go." Jase accepted the man's hand, and thanked him, before sliding the Le Mat back into his belt.

Jase left the fort that afternoon, preferring to spend the night in a solitary camp rather than around other people. He spent the next couple of weeks trading with the Indians on both the upper and lower reservations and whites in the surrounding areas. Through shrewd yet fair and honest trading, he had amassed enough furs and other goods that he had to hire a farmer with a wagon to transport them to Saint Paul.

Finding a good price, he had replenished the money in the pouch to a little more than when he first opened it. He was also owner of two good sized packs of trading goods that he felt could benefit him as he continued west. During his trading, he had traded the heavy army coat for a well-made buckskin shirt and a beaded sheath for a bowie-type belt knife he had bought. He also had acquired a long range Sharps rifle and cartridges because the Henry, while having rapid-firing abilities, was not known for its accuracy at long ranges.

Having previously just kept the Le Mat tucked in his belt, which did not work well at times, he decided to have a leather-worker make a holster that would fit behind his belt and keep the pistol handy for either right or left hand draw. While waiting for this to be made, he met a man that was heading for the gold fields in Montana territory. Finding that the man and some others were intending to travel with some troops that were advancing into

Dakota Territory, Jase decided to travel with them as part of his trade goods were aimed at miners.

Travel with the troops proved uneventful and they made good time until they reached the vicinity of Whitestone Hill in northern Dakota Territory. At this place the troops left the civilians and attacked an Indian village. The attack was without provocation and was very devastating to the Indians with women and children being killed. After the Indians fled, the soldiers destroyed everything left behind including food stores the Indians were building to get them through the coming winter.

After seeing the destruction and disregard for human life shown by the troops, Jase wanted no more to do with the military and made plans to leave. He made a deal with one of the gold seekers to buy his extra packhorse and the supplies he had intended to sell in the gold fields. Jase made no profit on this deal, but did get a return of his original investment. With the rest of his goods and his personal supplies loaded on the sorrel and riding the black he left the next day. Wanting just to be away from others, he headed south by west and began the trek that took him to Lake De Smet and the place of Jake's demise.

CHAPTER 10

Jase headed southwest of the lake and started the climb over the Big Horn Mountains. He followed a well-used trail that took him over hills and along a stream as it worked its way steadily up the mountain. He met no other travelers on the trail, but there were signs of a group of Indians traveling the same way. The track of the unshod horses and the drag marks of the travois appeared to be a day or two old.

As Jase gained in elevation, the coolness that came with it was a welcome relief from the oppressive heat of the low country. However, the coolness served as a reminder that fall was only a short time away. With it would come the early storms that are the start of the heavy snows that render these high mountains almost impassable.

As Jase was coming to the edge of a small valley high on the mountain, he caught the slight smell of wood smoke. Moving off the trail to a rise covered with trees, he could see a small Indian village. There were about twenty lodges grouped in the lush grass of the valley. As he studied the encampment through his telescope, he could see that it contained mostly women, children, and older men. He identified only eleven warriors in the whole camp and six of these appeared to be quite young. The camp seemed peaceful enough, so Jase decided to gamble contact with them.

Remembering a small heard of deer that he had seen a short distance back down the trail, Jase returned to the area where he saw them. They were still there, grazing in a clearing a short distance off the trail. Using the Henry, he dropped a large spike and two dry does. He took his time gutting them, then loaded the smaller of the does in front of the saddle on the black and started back to the trail.

He had just re-entered the trail and headed toward the Indian camp, when he spotted movement in the trees to his left front. He stopped and waited as four braves, probably a scouting party sent out at the sound of his shots, moved slowly forward while observing him and the surrounding country. He sat quietly with the Henry laid across the deer for easy use as the Indians approached. He did not readily recognize the tribe of Indians, but suspected they were Shoshoni.

Jase let the Indians approach and speak first. He was surprised when one of the Indians pointed at the deer, and then at him, and spoke in English, "Shoot --- You?" Jase nodded and said, "Two more back there --- You help?" As the Indian nodded, Jase turned his horses back down the trail. Two of the braves moved quickly into the lead. The brave that had spoken road alongside Jase as the fourth followed closely behind.

When they reached the place where Jase had re-entered the trail, the braves in the lead stopped and one pointed off the trail. Jase looked at the young man as if he did not know what he meant, then grinned and nodded. A slight smile crossed the brave's face at the affirmation of his tracking proficiency and with a whoop left the trail following Jase's previous tracks.

Finding the place where the deer lay, already gutted out, the brave next to Jase grinned, pointed at the pile of entrails, and said, "Woman's work." Jase shrugged and grinned back saying, "No woman," at which the braves all laughed. After loading the two deer, they road back to the Indian's camp together. As they road, Jase and the English speaking brave talked.

At first, Jase had some problem understanding the brave due to the Shoshoni's word order as compared to English, but soon picked up on the reversals. The brave, whose name was Tso'appeh, or Ghost, said he learned his English from a trapper that lived with them for a couple of years. He said that by description heard from others he knew of Jase as being a friend to the Indians. The Sioux said he had treated them fairly and though the Sioux were mostly enemies of the Shoshoni, word about him had spread. He said that among the Indians Jase was known as Bad Arm, or in the Shoshoni language, Peta Kaitsaan, which means, "arm that is no good."

Ghost also recognized the medallion as belonging to Jake. The old man was well known to the Shoshoni and was looked upon as being a friend. They called him Weihya Pampi, which means, Fire Hair. Jase told Ghost that Jake was his Grandfather, in the way of the Shoshoni, and that he had left Jase his medicine upon passing.

Ghost said Jase would be welcome in their village and, if he liked, he could travel with them to the Valley of the Warm Winds where they intended to winter. He added that their medicine man, and most of the warriors, took a different trail over the mountain. They were going to the big circle that is a place of great medicine to pray and ask for a good winter. The two bands were to meet where the water from the Ten Sleeps joins that of the Big Horn.

As they rode into camp, young boys and

girls came out to meet them. The others gathered around talking and looking at the white man. At a word from Ghost, some of the squaws took the deer Jase offered and quickly removing the hides, started preparing them for supper. As Jase unpacked and cared for his horses, three younger squaws, working under the direction of an older one, prepared a tipi for his use. Jase then laid out some of the trade items he felt might be of interest to the Indians.

He had gained a good degree of comfort in the camp, but was still wary and tried to keep a sharp eye. He had seen Ghost talking to others some yards into the camp and had just returned to his work when the man spoke almost in his ear. Spinning around and drawing his tomahawk as he turned, he looked into the grinning face of the Indian. He now knew how the Indian had come by his name. He had neither heard, nor felt the man approach, yet in what seemed only seconds, the man was there. Sliding the tomahawk back under his belt, Jase apologized for drawing a weapon on a friend as Ghost, in turn, apologized for approaching without warning.

Jase stayed with the Indians for a little over a week and traveled with them on over the mountain to a camp in a valley they called Ten Sleeps. The Indians intended to camp there a couple of days before heading to the Northwest to join the rest of their band. Jase traded some beads, trinkets, and cookware for some nicely tanned hides while with them. He also gave Ghost a good trade knife as a gift of their friendship.

Shortly after receiving the knife, Ghost took Jase with him to a place where they could overlook a clearing where five deer grazed. Leaving Jase with the horses, and all of his weapons except the knife, he told Jase to stay, look, and learn. Then staying low, out of sight of the deer, he moved to a position down wind of where they were grazing.

He spent a short time behind a large rock, just observing the deer. All of a sudden, Jase realized Ghost was standing about three steps in front of the rock with the knife in his hand. He was in plain view of the deer and one was looking directly at him, yet they never moved. The deer showed no alarm and continued to alternately graze and watch the surrounding area. Intently watching the whole scene, Jase realized that, though he had not seen the Indian move, Ghost had advanced a few steps closer to the deer.

Holding his telescope strictly on the Indian, he began to see the Indian's movements. With the upper part of the body staying always the same, only the feet moved. Ghost would stand perfectly still with his eyes intently watching the deer. At times he would take one, sometimes two steps forward and freeze again.

Jase moved his intent scrutiny to the deer. Though all seemed to be grazing, he realized that one or more would be watching the surroundings almost all the time. However, there was a second or two, at different times, when all heads would be down. Each time this happened, Ghost would be another step or two closer.

It took about forty-five minutes of patient progress before Ghost sprang astride his prey, a small buck, and with one swift movement reached around to slit its throat. After taking the deer to the ground, the Indian was up again dancing around his prize as the rest of the startled herd made the shelter of the trees. Leading the horses, Jase made his way down to congratulate his proud friend.

Ghost explained that sound, smell, and movement were the inbred keys most living things used to alert them of danger. Without these things, the mind often does not recognize what the eye sees. He showed how using this knowledge, along with a practiced blending with surroundings, allows the Indian to move unnoticed when there is reason to do so.

When the Indians broke camp to join the rest of their band, Jase continued on his separate trip. Ghost told him of a place where hot water flowed from the ground leaving formations of color on its way to the river, so he decided to find it. The place, Ghost said, laid Southwest of Ten Sleeps, so it was in the direction he was headed anyway. After crossing a stretch of desert to reach the Bighorn, he headed upstream, which took him southward, until he reached the hot springs.

There he found another band of Shoshoni swimming and bathing in the pools of warm water. Bringing greetings from Ghost, and wearing Jake's medallion, Jase was well accepted by this group also. He decided to spend a few days with these Indians trading and enjoying the warm springs.

The water came out of the ground at a temperature hot enough to cook with and some of the Indians were doing so. As the water reached catch ponds built by the Indians and natural indentures in the earth, minerals would line these places with color. The Indians would bath and just lie in these ponds enjoying their warmth. The water itself was believed to having healing properties on some illnesses and wounds. Jase actually felt the pain in his arm to be lessened after spending some time in the water. By the time he left, he found he could move his arm full motion with very little pain.

Following directions he received from the Indians, he crossed the river and started across the Owl Creek Mountains. Because the canyon cut through them by the river was virtually impassable, he went over a pass some distance to the West. Drifting through hills of red, he reached the summit and found the gradual decent into the Valley of the Warm Wind. From his position on the mountain, he could see a place where the river turned toward the West and he set his direction of travel toward this point.

Using a cleft in the far mountain for guidance, he crossed dry, arid country until he again came to the water that was now called the Wind River. Crossing the river at a place where it was joined by a smaller branch the Indians called the Popo Agie, he continued southwest up the lesser river. He soon reached some cabins that were a trading area built some years earlier by Captain Bonneville. He took this advantage to sell his pelts, hides and other things that he had gotten in trade and replenish his supplies.

A few settlers were building homesteads in the fertile valley and there was even talk of starting a settlement a few miles to the South. One settler told him that the crops grew so well that some were calling the area Push Root. He also warned that some of the Indians were starting to resent the whites and military in the area and there had been killings both ways. Gathering all the information he could about the area, and keeping the warnings in mind, Jase continued almost due South toward the head of the Popo Agie.

Following the river up canyon, he came to a place where it seemed to begin. It was a small pond that was filled with fish. The water seemed to come out of the ground from the bottom of the pond and seep from the ground all around. To his left, there were the washed boulders of a dry stream bed, but the river itself began at this pond. Taking time to enjoy the area, he was fishing a few yards down from the pond when he heard a faint shout.

Jase peered over the yellow brush as he studied the canyon carefully trying to find the shout's origin. There were a few green and yellow trees and some brush where the ground dropped off to the river downstream, but he could see no movement or anything out of place. As he changed position in his shelter, movement slightly to his left drew his attention. It was only an eagle diving toward what he felt was the river, which ran behind trees that were turning red by the change of the weather. Though he could not actually see the river, he could see the ground rising sharply from the other side.

It was covered with fir trees for about one hundred feet where it came to a solid rock wall that rose another hundred feet or more. It was a wall of gray rock that was layered like giant steps, with a few trees clinging precariously to the narrow ledges made by the steps. In many places, sections of the gray rock seemed to have fallen off leaving patches of reddish-brown scattered within the wall itself. Along the top, he could see a few trees and the remainder of an earlier snowfall that the sun had not yet melted away. The high snow reminded him that he might be facing some cold camps as he climbed higher up the mountain.

He was just contemplating the distance a small fire might be seen at night, when he saw figures moving along the face of the rim. The distance was so great that he could not make out what or who, it was, and his telescope was on the Black that was grazing by the pond. Watching until the figures disappeared beyond the rim, he decided it was most likely a small band of Indians. With the previous warnings in mind, he resolved to try to keep his movements concealed as much as possible.

Jase followed the dry stream bed up canyon some distance, when he heard the sound of water splashing over boulders. Quickly he moved his horses to higher ground, thinking he heard a flash flood coming toward him. Soon he could see the tumbling waters rushing toward the dry stream bed, yet it remained dry. It was as if the raging water just disappeared from the watercourse.

Still not trusting what his senses were telling him, he left his horses on higher ground and on foot worked his way toward the point where the water seemed to stop abruptly. At this point, the rushing water turned sharply toward the wall of the canyon. Slipping through the brush alongside the stream, he came to a cave like entrance at the bottom of the wall where the water just swirled and disappeared into it.

Pondering the phenomenon, Jase realized that the dry streambed was a course that part of the water would take if it reached greater volume than its regular course could handle. It appeared like the normal path was one that disappeared into the bowls of the earth at this point and resurfaced again at the pond further down the canyon. The path it took getting there was one that only God and the fish would know.

Jase worked his way further up the canyon above deeply cut gorges cut by the stream as it raced toward the valley. Reaching a place where the water ran only a few feet below him, he stopped for the night. Having seen nothing of the Indians he had spotted while at the pond, he found a sheltered spot and built a small fire. As he cooked two of the fish he caught at the pond, he marveled at the nature around him.

The place he had chosen gave him a view of the stream cascading down the rock wall from some distance above him. Sections of the stream took different paths as each splashed and sprayed from the rocks as it fell. Here in this beautiful place of nature, Jase attempted to make plans for his future. Up to this time, his travels were guided mainly by a deep need to distance himself from the turmoil in the East.

The war had taken away his beloved wife and the life they had together on the plantation. He did not know the status of Brian and his family, whether his father's old place was still standing, or had met the same fate as the plantation. He decided to try to contact Brian by letter as soon as he found a place to settle at least long enough for return mail to find him. With this in mind, he decided to try to find a place to perhaps plant some roots somewhere in the Oregon country.

According to information he had gleaned from the Indians and whites he had met, his present path should bisect the new section of the Oregon Trail known as the Lander Cutoff. This was the first time since he received the information about the massacre at the plantation, that he had given any thought about any kind of future for himself. With this planning, came a lightness of heart and the beginning of a determination to see these plans through.

With a new focus, he set out along a steep trail that ran along the West edge of the falls. He even took time to bath in a pool that was fed by a trickle of water that escaped from the roaring stream. Even in this relaxed time, he stayed wary as the framework of a lodge that stood close by showed the place to be one often frequented by Indians.

He continued South through high mountain valleys, past lakes, and over ridges of timber. After reaching a more barren part of the mountain, he crossed a ridge and saw a wagon train in the distance. As he watched the wagons moving slowly alongside a stream, he felt sure he had reached the Lander Cutoff.

The wagons had circled and made camp for the evening by the time Jase intercepted them. As he drew close, the wagon boss and a couple of others rode out to meet him. After talking with him, and finding out his intent of traveling to Oregon by the same route, they invited Jase to join them. Even though it was a large train, another able-bodied man would be a welcome addition.

As they entered the camp, Jase was surprised to see a small contingent of Negroes within the ranks of the train. He was caring for his horses and gear not far from them, when he noticed two of the Negro men approaching. One of the men stated, "Wen yous gits set, wees got plenty of vittles ifen yous would care to join us." As Jase turned to face them in the fading light, the man threw up his hands an almost screamed, "Lordy be, I sees a gose." "Massa Jase" he exclaimed wide eyed, "I knows it be you, is yous live, or is I a talking to the dead?"

Even with the ugly burn scare on the side of the man's face, Jase recognized Thomas, who had been one of the overseers on the plantation. The man with him, he knew, was Will another of their former slaves. After assuring Thomas and Will that he was alive and not a ghost, he joined them for supper.

Jase recognized all in the small group, except two little ones, as former slaves at the plantation. Mable, Will's wife, gave him a hug and stated, "I can't believe what I sees, Missy, she be missing you so much." Then added, "She be so glad to see you." Jase, still somewhat stunned at finding the former slaves, took a minute for the implication of what she said to register.

As realization set in, he grabbed the woman's shoulders in both hands and asked, "Priscilla, she's alive ----- She's here?" "Oh yes sir, Massa Jason, she be live, but she not here," the woman answered. "She an Massa Burleigh, they be back at the South Pass Station," Thomas said. "Massa Burleigh, he be feeling poorly, they stay there and send us on ahead." Will stated, adding "Ira n Bartholomew, they stay with them.

In a form of shock at the news, Jase almost mounted the Black and headed into the night to find his beloved wife. However, his better judgment won out and he decided to leave after first light in the morning. During supper, and for some time after, Jase told his story, and listened intently as the Negroes told theirs.

Burl had given all the slaves the papers that gave them their freedom. However only three left the plantation and these only to find family from whom they had been separated. The plantation was in good shape with most of the crops going to supply the war effort.

One evening, about an hour before dark, the Yankees attacked. First shells from the big guns hit the main house and some of the other buildings. Then, the soldiers came with torches burning buildings and crops alike. Many that tried to fight back were killed or wounded. The burns on Thomas' face came from one of the torches as he tried to stop a raider from firing the main barn.

Burl's wife, Susannah, and two of the Negroes were killed when the first shell hit the house and Burl was wounded and knocked unconscious. Some of the former slaves, Will included, pulled Burl from the burning house and hid with him in the woods. Priscilla had been working with three of the Negro children on their reading alongside a creek than ran a short distance from her and Jase's small house. First hiding under a bridge, when the chance arose, they headed for the relative safety of the woods.

It was a full day before Burl regained consciousness and another day before he was able to travel. They then returned to the ruin of the plantation. Priscilla, and the children, had found refuge with a Free Black family at their small cabin a couple of miles away. They returned the day after Burl and the others. The neighbors first thought all were killed, thus the word Jase had received.

Burl, Priscilla, and the Negroes buried their dead and salvaged enough from the ruin of the plantation to stay on for a while. However, when word came that Jase was killed in a battle far to the North, Priscilla wanted to leave. Burl, his wife gone and all he had worked for in ruin, agreed with his daughter's wish to move further West away from the invading army. Repairing what wagons they could, they and some of the Negroes joined with others that were moving westward into Kansas. After staying in Kansas a few months, with the war ever close and Burl's health improving, the decision was made to head for Oregon.

On the trip along the Sweetwater and over South Pass, Burl again became ill. When they reached South Pass Station, the wagon train rested a couple of days while feeding their stock on the lush grass. On the second day, a rider came through and told of a doctor that was headed back east. He said that the doctor should make it to South Pass in three or four more days. Priscilla, worried about her father, made the decision to stay at the station and wait for the doctor even though the rest of the train had to move on.

All of the former slaves, along with two other white families that had traveled with them, intended to stay also. However, at Burl's request, it was decided that Priscilla, Burl, and the two Negro men would keep two of the wagons and wait for the doctor. The other Negroes would take the other six wagons and continue on with the train. Their friends with the other two wagons would help the Negroes find a place and all would setup a small community once they got to Oregon.

The commander of the small contingent of soldiers stationed at South Pass Station said he had word that another wagon train was traveling about a week behind them. The last two wagons would try to join that train and continue the trip after the doctor had seen Burl. That way all would be traveling with others along the trail and the two wagons would have protection while at the station.

Jase had noticed two riders come in from the West a short time after dark the night before. However, as they had bed down with another part of the train, he had paid them little mind. He was saddled, packed, and ready to go a little after first light and had just joined Thomas and the others for a quick breakfast when the two men came over. He was surprised to see that both were dark skinned. One looked to be a Mulatto and the other of full Negro decent.

Finding that the train was heading to Oregon and contained some Free Blacks, the men felt obliged to share their experiences. They also were Free Blacks and like these, they had joined a wagon train and headed for Oregon. When they arrived, they found that the Oregon constitution that was drawn up in 1857 prohibited Free Blacks, whether they were part or full Negro, to live in the state. Pressure was put on them to leave and when their white friends tried to help them, they too had problems with the law. With the threat of a whipping and fearing reprisals on their friends, they sold their meager belongings and headed back over the trail.

With this new information, it was decided that the Negroes would bid their friends in the train good bye and turn their four wagons back toward South Pass. Jase, anxious to see Priscilla and Burl, would leave his packhorse with them and ride on ahead. Back at South Pass, while they were waiting for the doctor to come through, they would decide on another destination where perhaps they all would be welcome.

W. C. Dick

Chapter 11

The wagon train had been gone a day and Burl was resting peacefully, except for occasional coughing. Priscilla worried over her father's condition as he had gotten much worse over the last week. He had never regained his former health after the slaves pulled him from the burning wreckage of their former house, and often had problems breathing. However, this time he seemed to struggle for each breath, and had become so weak he could hardly talk.

As Ira brought some broth to feed his former master, Priscilla thanked God for the devotion of their extended slave family. Ira had been one of those that had pulled Burl from the crumbling house, and had never been over a shout away from him since. Bartholomew, the other former slave that had stayed behind with them, gave her a bowl of stew as she exited the wagon. They sat together eating and watched the sun sink into the hills beyond the small army post. As the soldiers lowered the flag in the parade ground, her thoughts went back to Jase and the plantation. This war had cost them so much.

Revile had come early in the post, and Priscilla was awakened by the sound of the troops making ready for travel. The telegrapher from St Mary's Station had wired for help as a band of Indians was making trouble further down the Sweetwater. The telegrapher and two other troopers would be left to man the South Pass Station and the other troops would go down river to help. However, no problems were expected, as no other Indians were known to be in this area.

Red Broine watched the troops leave from his vantage point in the willows below the station. Corbett had sent him to try to find out what was going on after they heard the early revile. Though Red had not gotten close enough to hear actual conversations, he saw and heard enough to have a good idea of what was happening. He knew the troops would be gone a day, or longer, and only three men would be guarding the post. When he took this information back to the other four waiting men, they came alive with anticipation.

Roland Corbett had lost two good men in a brush with the law down Colorado way. One of these was Bull Cortland his friend from youth. Bull had been his right arm, and they had always watched each other's back. The four men he had left were all tough men, but he had little trust in any of them and could call none a friend.

The fire haired boy they called Red was a Texas cowboy that had joined him after killing a man in a saloon brawl. He was an able hand, but was prone to acting without thinking. His lack of patience had been one of the reasons things had gone awry in Colorado.

Cully Rasmusson was a once proud fighter that had ridden with J. E. B. Stuart's Cavalry. He lost faith in himself when, out of ammunition, he broke and ran during a heavy battle. Running from what he felt was his own cowardice, he joined Corbett's crew. Although he cringed at Corbett's ruthlessness, he stayed with him and was always in the forefront of any fight

Rhondy Mitchell was driven by greed and would do most anything for a dollar. In his forty-seven years, he had killed six men and two women, all for personal gain. Having no conscience or regard for others, he fit well with Corbett's outlaws. Although, with chance of profit, he was always willing to do Corbett's bidding, Roland never showed the man his back.

Leon Vasquez had been with him the longest and was probably the most loyal. Roland had saved the Mexican from a hanging shortly after leaving Kansas and the man felt he owed Corbett his life. Leon, having seen his family killed by "good people' as a child, had little respect for the lives of others.

Leaving the Colorado law behind, the outlaws headed north for the gold fields in Montana. Robbing miners would be easier in that less settled area. Roland, however, had some qualms about returning to the North Country, as that was where he had last heard about the old man that was dogging his trail.

He had first heard of the old man when he was leaving Kansas. Having little fear of any man, his first instinct was to find the old man and shoot him on sight. He had only a description of the old man and the distinctive medallion he wore, but had not seen him personally except in his dreams. In these dreams, the old man would never die but would just keep coming. Roland developed a belief that if they ever met, it would be his life that came to an end rather than that of the old man. However, after not hearing anything about the old man for most of a year, the uneasiness had subsided, though it was not totally gone.

Though the small group had money, the fear of being recognized kept them away from the normal supply points, and as they approached South Pass Station their supplies were about gone. Seeing the two wagons staying behind as the train pulled out gave Corbett an idea. Two wagons traveling alone would be easy prey.

Though they could not go near the station with the soldiers there, they had but to wait and see which of the three trails the wagons took. Then they could easily be taken and besides the needed supplies, there may be other things of value. Corbett had also seen the pretty, blond girl and was having ideas of what he might do with her.

After watching the wagons and post all day, and seeing no signs that the wagons were readying to pull out, the outlaws' spirits were quite low as night fell. Corbett especially was very remorse as he had been dwelling on how much he was going to enjoy the blond that was with the wagons. He kept one person on watch for a chance to slip up on the wagons during the night. This chance was not to come, as one of the two Negroes with the wagons was awake all night. In addition, the bright full moon would make any movement easily seen by the sentries who were taking turns in the sentinel box on the roof of the stable.

The news of the troops moving out gave hope to their plan. Three troopers could be easily taken if they planned carefully, and then they would take the wagons. By killing them all, no one would know they were responsible, and if they burned the post, blame would most likely be put on the Indians.

Waiting long enough for the troops to have gained enough distance that shots could not be heard, the men approached the post as though they were coming down the trail from the West. They rode to the small gate on the west side of the post, exchanging friendly waves and words with the trooper in the sentinel box. Four of the men dismounted tying their horses at the gate. Rhondy, using unseen movements of spurs and reins, caused his horse to act-up. Making a comment about his "nag" wanting water, he rode alongside the long building out of view of the sentry.

Reaching the other end of the building, he dismounted. He then made his way to a back door and through the empty kitchen until he had a view of the parade ground opposite his comrades. The Sargent that was left in charge of the post stood in the middle of the small parade ground talking with Corbett and the others.

On cue from Corbett, Rhondy shot the Sargent in the back. At the same time, Red and Cully turned and shot the sentry in the box as Roland and Leon put bullets into the telegrapher that was standing just outside his door. As they made a quick check to make sure the soldiers were dead and no others were in the compound, Rhondy looked out the main gate toward the wagons. Seeing one of the Negroes heading from one wagon to the other with his arms full of rifles and gear, he raised his rifle and dropped him in his tracks.

Bartholomew was in the wagon where the two Negroes slept when the gunfire started. Grabbing the rifles that were there, along with shot and powder, he started for the other wagon. He had taken but a few steps when Rhondy's bullet clipped one of the rifles he was carrying and shattered his heart. Ira's quick shot, though a second too late, sent the outlaw diving behind the thick fence as it burned across his back.

Corbett sent his men to positions throughout the post where they would have five points from which to fire on the wagon. He ordered all to take caution with their shots, as he did not want the woman hit. He had other plans for her. However, after a short exchange of shots, it became quite clear that the wagon would not be easily taken. The occupants were well barricaded in and both the Negro and the woman were very good shots.

Deciding that some other plan would

have to be put in place if they were to take the wagon, Corbett was looking for a way to get men into position behind the wagon. His planning was interrupted by a shout from Red. From his position in the sentinel box, his keen eyes had seen a rider far to the West. Corbett moved to the high vantage point and together he and Red watched the rider coming their way at a fast lope. Knowing that a man riding alone in this country would have to have some savvy, they decided he could present a problem. Besides that, the speed and direction he was traveling indicated the post as being his destination. He would have to be taken out as he reached there, with no warning and without the chance for a miss.

After positioning the dead sentry's body in a natural position, complete with carbine, Corbett took the man's extra ammo and left Red to keep tabs on the rider. Moving Cully from the stable door to the small western gate, he gave both men orders to take no chances on a miss, unless the rider was warned by those in the wagon. Corbett then went back to the room behind the telegraph office.

With Vasquez in the room further to the south, and Rhondy at the main gate, they still had the wagon well covered. Corbett felt he had found a way to get one of his men behind the second wagon and another some distance behind the occupied one. Once the rider was out of the way, it should not be long before the wagons and the woman would be his.

In the wagon, Ira and Priscilla hunkered behind their barricade, rifles in hand. Burl was propped partially upright behind them with their third rifle ready. Being too unstable to shoot straight, he was attempting to keep their three rifles loaded and ready to fire. Most of their shot and powder, however, had been in the other wagon and now lay on the ground between them along with Bartholomew. Trying not to waste shots, they were able to keep two guns loaded most of the time. They were well aware though that, with only three muzzle-loading rifles, if they were rushed it would all be over.

Hearing Red's call about the rider stirred a glimmer of hope. However, as they heard bits and pieces of the plan to ambush him, their hope slowly faded. They decided that they would have to warn the rider. Warning shots would be the only way, but they would have to be timed so the rider would be close enough to recognize a problem without being so close as to be a good target. The problem was that they could only depend on their ears to let them know the location of the rider as the buildings and fence of the post blocked any view.

Realizing that they occasionally got a glimpse of the hat worn by the outlaw in the tower, they made a decision. At the first sign of the hat, after they began to hear hoof beats, they would both fire at it. This would put the rider on the alert and perhaps take out one of the shooters. With this decided, they held their rifles ready and settled down to wait and listen.

As the slight breeze brought the faint sound of hoof beats, both Ira and Priscilla raised their rifles. A small portion of the hat was visible, but not enough for a target. Before they could see enough of the hat to perhaps hit it, they heard Red's warning. "He is staying high," the lookout said, "he is either going by or around to the front gate." "Cully, you watch this side, I'm going to the stable door" the red head said as he went down the ladder. Changing his attention to the stable door as the hoof beats were becoming louder, Ira saw the outlaw just as the rider cleared the edge of the building.

Ira squeezed off his shot a second before something hit his shoulder knocking him flat in the wagon, almost on top of Burl. He heard Priscilla's shot that sent splinters into Leon's face, and saw her trade Burl for their last loaded rifle. Moving to a sitting position beside Burl, he began to load the rifle that he had with one hand. He had not seen the results of his shot, but surmised the rider was still alive when he heard an exchange of fire from within the building.

As Jase and the Black moved eastward at a fast lope, he heard a couple shots in the distance. Being ever on the alert, he watched the hills and valleys for any sign of movement. Seeing a heard of antelope run over a hill far to his right front, he gave the sound to be shots from a hunter. About this time, he could barely make out some structures that had to be South Pass Station. Later as he started down the grade toward the Sweet Water, he could see the tops of two wagons on the opposite side of the post.

Jase's heart thumped and his breath came quicker as he thought of seeing Priscilla. He was barely aware of the sentry in the box and the flag moving gently over the quiet post. Although he noticed horses tied on the west side of the post, being intent on the wagons on the other side, he kept the Black to the road above it. The Black slowed only slightly as Jase turned him off the road toward the corner of the stable. Eyes and mind intent on the wagons, Jase rounded the corner of the stable.

A woman's scream of "watch out" was nearly drowned out by the almost simultaneous roars of a rifle and pistol.

The black turned sharp left causing Jase to lose the saddle and tumble to the ground. Two more rifle shots rang out as Jase sprang to his feet, colt in hand. Three quick steps took him past a red haired man that lay dead in the doorway, and into the stable. Ira's shot had torn through Red's body just as he had triggered his pistol. The impact caused the shot to miss, grazing the neck of the black causing him to bolt. The last thing Red saw was the rider falling from his horse, and his last thought was "got him."

Jase moved to the side of the doorway and crouched behind the post of a stall while he let his eyes adjust to the darkness. From the other side of the doorway that led into the inner stable that bordered the parade ground, a voice called " Red ---- Red, you get him?" Jase answered, "He's dead, and you're fixing to be." The man muttered something Jase could not make out, and when Jase heard a movement, he sent a shot in that direction. The man fired a wild return shot and Jase heard him run out of the building.

Cully shouted the news that Red was dead and had missed the rider as he ran to the officer's quarters in the long building that made up the West side of the post. Corbett cussed, then said "We'll get him, Vasquez got the nigger." Jase recognized the voice, but could not place to whom it belonged. He decided, however, that he should contact Priscilla, and the others in the wagon, to find out what was going on.

Moving to a place by the door where he could see the wagons, he studied the view. There was the body of a dead Negro lying between the wagons amongst some rifles and gear, but he could see no one else. The closer wagon had the cover pulled up a couple of inches above the side, and he could barely make out the business end of a rifle sticking out. Gambling a look down the side of the compound, he could see nothing as the fence blocked his view of the other buildings.

Staying well inside the building so he could keep his eyes adjusted to the dark, he shouted Priscilla's name. Watching the other door to the stable, he waited for what seemed an eternity before the questioning answer came. "Ja ---- who is that" came Priscilla's unsure voice. "It's Jase honey," he answered, "I'm here." "Jason? --- I thought you were dead" she stammered. "And I you" Jase returned, "We'll talk about that later." "Where are the troops and what is going on?" Jase asked.

After Priscilla gave a brief explanation of the situation, Ira added, "You do wat you has to Massa Jason, I'll take care of Missy and Massa Burl." At the sound of Ira's voice, Corbett let out a string of cuss words. "I hit that black bastard, I know I did" Leon said. "Well you didn't hit him good enough" Corbett growled. Jase reached up and fingered Jake's medallion as the voice drew him back to the events so long ago. He knew to whom the voice belonged.

Remembering that Jake had hounded Corbett until the old man's death, Jase decided to give Roland more to think about. A rattled man makes mistakes. As Jase cautiously made his way to the inner stable, he taunted Corbett. "Roland Corbett, old Jake sends his regards," Jase hollered. "Who the hell are you" Corbett asked? "I'm your worst nightmare Corbett" Jase answered, "Me and the old man's spirit that is." Corbett's men knew about the old man, and a chill went through all. The Mexican, Vasquez, even crossed himself in the way of the Catholic.

Three windows and a doorway along the inner stable gave Jase assorted views of the parade ground and other buildings yet allowed him to stay quite well hidden from view. Due to seeing the four horses by the small gate and the other one at the other end of the long building, Jase was sure he was dealing with five men. Red lay dead behind him, and after some time watching, he knew the locations of the other four.

One was behind the heavy main gate that was half open, in the fence that made up the eastern side of the compound. Another was in the closest room, of the three, in the long section of building on the West. The other two were in the room at the Southeast corner of the parade ground. Glimpses of the two through the doorway and lone window of the room, led Jase to believe they were alternating between there and a position deeper in the building where they could watch the wagon.

With no changes in these locations after some time, Jase believed the outlaws had trapped themselves in places they could not exit without exposing themselves to fire from either he or those in the wagon. Changing his location often, Jase was able to keep a close watch without exposing himself. He had taken shots only when he felt he had a reasonable target, but had done little damage. However, none of the shots taken by the outlaws had even come close.

Seeing movement in the window across the parade ground, Jase fired. The hammer of the colt clicked on an empty chamber. At the sound of the empty gun, Rhondy Mitchell smelled blood. He stepped out from behind the gate with both guns blazing fire at the doorway where Jase had been.

Drawing the Le Matt as he moved to a window, Jase put two bullets into the man and one each into the doorways of the two buildings before the outlaws could spot his position. Rhondy grabbed the half-closed gate for support when he was hit, and as he went down, he swung the gate wide open. A rifle barked from the wagon, and Cully Rasmusson slid down the doorjamb of the officers' quarters. He just sat there holding his stomach.

Three down, Jase thought, but the other two were well barricaded in the corner building and could not be easily hit. Jase realized he only had five shots left in the nine shot Le Matt, and his reloading equipment was on the Black along with the Henry rifle. The red head had cartridges in his belt, but Jase remembered that his revolver had landed well out in the open and could not be reached without exposure to fire. As he looked out over the parade ground, and the bodies of the outlaw and two soldiers, he remembered noticing that the soldier in the sentinel box still had his carbine.

Climbing the ladder, he found the carbine still propped alongside the dead body of the guard. However, a quick search revealed that his extra ammunition was gone. Carefully sliding the rifle down, he found that the round in the chamber was intact, so that would give him one shot. Peering over the edge of the box, he found that the higher elevation gave him a little better view into the room. Just below the window, he could make out the top of a man's head and part of the brim of the sombrero hanging from his back. Sliding the carbine over the edge of the box, he took and held steady aim.

Leon Vasquez was thinking about the choices he had made that had led him to this place as he moved a bit higher to look across the compound. Those were his last thoughts as the heavy bullet blew pieces of his brain into the room behind him. Corbett, watching the wagon from that room, heard the rifle shot and Leon's body crumple to the floor. However, it was the smell of blood that drove home the fact that he was now trapped and alone. Driven by fear, he bolted out the door and ran for the rear of the building.

Ira held the rifle in his good arm, while Priscilla worked on the wound in his other shoulder. The rifle shot from the sentinel box surprised them both, and their attention was there at the time Corbett ran. Ira caught the movement, swung the rifle, and fired. His bullet splintered wood as Corbett disappeared around the edge of the building. Priscilla shouted to Jase, "One ran around back, watch him."

Jase was sure of his hit, but was watching the corner room for any movement when Ira's rifle barked. At Priscilla's shout, he thought about the horse he had seen tied at the rear of the long building. He rolled over the edge of the sentinel box and keeping it between him and the corner room, he moved to the edge of the roof. Even there, the west side building blocked his view of the horse. Dropping to the ground, he moved into the open.

About fifty feet away he could see hands working to free the reins from where they were tied around the end of a building log. He could also hear Corbett cussing the frightened horse for pulling tightly against the reins. He fired at the hands, and missed. A second shot burned wood just as the reins came loose. The horse reared pulling free, and, with reins flying, took off on a frightened run for the river.

Flattening against the wall, Jase worked his way to where the horse had stood. Peering around the edge, he could see two of the corners of the three sections of buildings that made up the southern edge of the post. From his previous vantage point on the roof, he had been able to get a reasonably good idea of the layout of this section of the post.

A sign he had seen over the door of the building closest to him identified it as the commissary. It was one end of the long building that bordered the parade ground. The other end was the building the two outlaws were in. The telegraph wire running from a pole to the side of it, and the eye shade still on the dead man in front of it, gave clue that it was the telegrapher's office and quarters.

Between the two was a longer room Jase felt might be the mess hall. His reasoning for that was the stove pipe extending from the roof of the section of building that jutted out twenty or so feet to the rear. He had no idea of the use of the section behind the telegraph office that shared the wall with the kitchen. It extended another ten or twelve feet beyond the kitchen, but he was sure it had no rear door. That meant that any entrance back into the post from this area would have to be through either the kitchen or the commissary.

Moving to the side of the commissary, Jase drew no fire and saw nothing. As he peered around that corner, a bullet thudded into the wall scant inches from his head. Returning a shot at a piece of shirt barely visible at the corner of the kitchen, he watched and waited. Making sure there was no door or window at the rear of the commissary, he moved swiftly to the wall of the kitchen. Just as he began this move, he heard the sound of boots on a wooden floor.

Rounding the corner, he could see the lone door on that end of the post leading into the kitchen. Moving up beside it, he stood listening. He could hear nothing, then from deep inside the room a slight scraping sound such as a piece of furniture being bumped or moved was heard, and then again silence. The half-closed door, however, blocked any view into the room.

Bunching his muscles, he sprang across the door opening to the other side. The expected shot never came. Cautiously peering into the room from this side of the door, he could see the corner of the big stove, but not much else. The space around that corner of stove would afford protection, if he could reach it. Diving to the floor, he rolled to a crouch behind the stove as a bullet imbedded its self into the wall above him.

Looking around Jase spotted a broom that stood in the corner. Reached out with a toe and hooking it around the broom, he jerked it toward him. At the movement, a shot ricocheted off the front of the stove and ruined a portion of the doorjamb. Reaching with the broom, he closed the door leaving his end of the room in darkness.

After letting his eyes adjust, he took careful glances beyond the stove. He could see no hiding places in the room other than the far side of the big stove, but was sure the shots had not come from that close. The room beyond was well lit, but showed little. Through the doorway, he could only see a desk, chair, the corner of a table, and the open window.

Other than the shots, Jase had heard no movement since entering the building and thinking the shots may have came from the window, Jase realized Corbett could be heading for the horses at the back gate. Even worse, he might surprise those in the wagon. Springing to his feet, Jase ran for the doorway.

Too late, he remembered the scraping sound he had heard before he entered the kitchen. Splinters and fire erupted from the desk as a blow to the hip started him falling to the floor. Firing his last two rounds into the desk as he was going down, he clicked on an empty chamber as he hit the floor.

Corbett stood up from behind the desk, blood starting to seep through his shirt from the slight wound in his side. Jase cocked the Le Matt, and reached with his left as though to hold the pistol in both hands. The movement was silent as he tipped the front part of the hammer downward.

"Yours is empty, mines not" Corbett growled as he raised his pistol. Then with his inherent need to inflict pain, he grinned and added, "Then I am going to have my way with that pretty little filly in the wagon." The whine of a bullet whizzing by and the sound of a pistol shot made him duck. The roar was deafening as the load of buckshot aimed for his chest ripped apart his throat. The impact slammed him to his back with the evil grin still on his face.

Jase gained his feet and limped around the desk, knife in hand. With one look, he returned the knife to its sheath and removed the still cocked revolver from the Corbett's dead hand. Looking out the window, he saw the gut-shot man propped against the doorframe of the officers' quarters. The man was holding a pistol with both hands and appeared to be trying to cock it. As he saw Jase, a smile crossed his face and he tried to throw the pistol away. He only succeeded in dropping it by his side.

Jase checked the loads in the revolver, and limped out the door to check on the man in the telegraph office. Seeing the dead Mexican on the floor, he shouted to Priscilla that it was all over, and headed for the man in the doorway. As he drew close, the man stated, "It's a Le Matt ain't it?" At Jase's nod, the man began to talk.

"When I heerd that blast I knowed it," he said. "I used to ride with Jeb Stuart and seed hisn," he continued with pride in his shaky voice. "That Le Matt, she's the onsly gun I ever seed with a shot gun in the middle," he expounded. "Still had my pride in them days, a riding with Stuart," he proceeded, then added "Mam" with a nod as Priscilla walked up.

Putting his arm around Priscilla, Jase ask, "You shot at Corbett, why?" Cully coughed and blood seeped from the corners of his mouth. Finally he answered, "Corbett was an animal, he were no good." He had another coughing spell then continued, "My Mama, she raised me right an I let her down." "I'm dying, going to join Mama," he stated weakly, then added, "Had to do one last thing right."

"Couldn't let him git to the Lady," he stammered as he raised his hand toward Priscilla. The hand slowly dropped and Cully Rasmusson left this world in peace.

Chapter 12

Jase and Pricilla held each other tightly and kissed for a long moment. Their emotions at being together, after each believing the other dead, were almost overwhelming. A call from Ira, who was watching from the wagon, finally brought them back to a world not just their own. Hand in hand they walked to the wagon with the Black following close behind after he spotted Jase.

Hearing both Ira and Burl talking as they walked up, Jase assumed that they were reasonably well. He then turned and walked to the still body of Bartholomew. The faithful former slave had not moved from where he fell and Jase felt that his life had left him before he hit the ground. Automatically gathering the weapons that Bartholomew had been carrying, Jase returned to the wagon. Ira met him with a big grin stating "It shore good to see you Massa Jase, you the best looking dead man I ever did see." Tears streaming down his cheeks, Burl tried to rise and throw his arms around Jase's neck. Jase knelt beside the weak old man and accepted his unusual show of emotion

Realizing the strain the old man had been under with his fear for his daughter and being ill enough that he could do little to protect her, Jase stayed and talked with him for a while. Pricilla started a small fire as Ira got slowly out of the wagon and helped her put water on to boil. Ira then went to the body of his dead friend Bartholomew, covered him with a blanket and said some parting words to him. As the water was heating Jase went to the Black to retrieve some of the herbs from his saddle bags. The Black nuzzled him a gentle greeting as he walked up, but shied slightly at the smell of the blood on his leg.

Jase mixed some of the herbs into a cup of the water as Pricilla mixed others into a poultice according to Jase's instructions. Burl was given the herb tea to drink and the poultice was used on both Ira's and Jase's wounds. The bullet that had knocked Jase down had been turned by the heavy leather of the colt's holster enough so that it went through the muscle but missed the bone. Pricilla had just finished applying the poultice and bandage to Jase's leg when the sound of a bugle broke the stillness.

The detachment of troops came into the station riding slowly and alert for trouble. A dispatch rider had met them before they reached St Mary's Station and informed them that the Indian problem had been resolved so they could return to their own post. A scout riding in advance of the troops heard some of the gunfire from the station and reported back. They rode hard until close to the station and when their bugle call brought no return they rode in slowly and ready for trouble.

After looking the situation over, the Captain took statements from Jase, Pricilla, and Ira as his troops tended to the dead and cleaned up the aftermath of the fight. A call of "Wagons" from one of the solders heralded the arrival of Thomas and the others. After greetings and explanations of the fight at the station, two of the former slaves began preparing their dead brother, Bartholomew, for burial. Three of the women began a meal while the rest of the group helped the soldiers.

Bartholomew and the soldiers were each given a proper burial, but on order of the Captain, the outlaws were put in a common grave away from the others. It was only due to the persistence of Jase and those of his party that words were read over them. So intense was the soldier's hatred over the ambush of their comrades that some were seen spitting on the grave as they left.

The herbs Jase was giving Burl seemed

to be helping him and he was able to attend the burial. He was even participating in much of the socializing around the camp by the time the doctor arrived three days later. However, Jase was about out of the herb.

The Doctor said that the heat and smoke of the fire had damaged Burl's lungs quite badly. He recommended treatments requiring the breathing of steam laced with medication three times a day. He supplied enough medication to make the trip to Fort Bridger where more could be acquired. The only drawback being that a stop would have to be made mid-day of travel to build a fire to heat the water. It was time to travel on, and the decision was made to start the trail for Fort Bridger and look for land to the West of there. Adding the outlaw's horses to the livestock they already had, and taking leave of those at the station, the small group of wagons headed west.

Three days out Jase had stopped the wagons for the noon meal and Burl's treatment. Most of the wagons were drawn into a half circle in order to shelter the fire from a brisk north wind. Thomas and the two men from Oregon were just returning with a wagon loaded with water barrels they had filled from a clear stream that ran a quarter mile to the south.   Burl had finished his breathing treatment and was just starting into a plate of meat and beans as he watched the men returning from the stream. Choking from trying to swallow and shout at the same time, his gravelly voice finally got out the word "Indians!" Gathering on a rise across the stream was a group of Indians.

At Burl's warning, the men on the wagon swung it into a position where it stood between the other wagons and the stream.   Quick repositioning of the two end wagons completed a reasonable circle. The stock was unhitched and brought to the center of the circle and gaps between the wagons were filled with trunks and other items that would provide some shelter. Guns and ammunition were laid out before the meal was finished and they set down to wait. The Indians were all male and sporting war paint, so they knew they were in for a fight.

Jase studied the Indians as they made their way down the bank into the hidden shelter of the stream. They looked like Shoshoni, yet were enough different from those he had met that he could not be sure. Perhaps they are a different band. Most carried only bow, arrow and lance, but half-a-dozen carried rifles.

The Indians remained out of sight for some time, and then came out of the streambed yelling and whooping. They were in two bunches, one east of the wagons and one to the west. Riding hard in single file, the groups merged into a solid line encircling the wagons. Those within the circle of wagons waited until Jase gave the word then opened fire in a single volley. Five of the Indians fell from their horses and two others slumped over but stayed astride their mounts. One horse went down pitching its rider off, but the Indian quickly disappeared into a fold in the earth. Switching weapons, another volley from the wagons left two more horses' rider less as the Indians broke for the shelter of the creek bank.

Those in the wagons were amazed at the amount of arrows imbedded in the wagons and other items for such a short battle. They were lucky that the only injury was an arrow through the shoulder of one of the women that was loading rifles. None of the Indian's rifles seemed to have hit their mark. Though painful, the woman's wound was soon bandaged and she was back helping prepare for another attack. Watching the stream bank closely, they reinforced barricades and filled buckets and pans with water in case the Indians used fire arrows.

It was Eugenia, the Negro woman that had been struck by the arrow, who first saw

Indian movement. She caught brief sight of a brave as he slithered over the bank to disappear behind a clump of sagebrush. Others then caught slight movements now and again but only briefly. Jase had used the Henry during the attack, but the Sharps was loaded and ready. Picking up the sharps he waited while Ira studied the areas where movement had been seen through the telescope. Spotting a bit of red war paint through a clump of sage, he directed Jase to it. Setting the sites on the center of the brush, Jase touched off the big gun. The Indian was seen only slightly as he was thrown backward along with bits of sage. Ira reported seeing only part of an unmoving foot as Jase reloaded.

Jase spotted a head peering over the bank toward the Indian he had just shot. Just as he squeezed the set trigger the head disappeared. Holding his gaze on the top of the bank he caught the head again peering over the bank closer to the dead Indian. Adjusting his site on the new target the Sharps spoke again. With the boom of the gun, parts of the Indian's head could be seen flying off as the head disappeared. Shouts and calls between the Indians seemed to slow their movements and heighten their caution. They had not given up and were still moving slowly toward the wagons as was evident by occasional quick glimpses of brown skin. None however long enough to supply a target.

Most in the wagons were intently watching for the Indian's movements between the wagons and the stream and on both east and west flanks. Their concentration was broken by Will, who was guarding the north side of the wagons. His exclamation of "Lord have mercy" caused all to turn toward him. As gazes continued past him others began to mutter and cries of shock escaped the lips of a few. An even larger group of mounted Indians had appeared to the north and just sat on their horses, watching from a distance.

A cry from Ira "Their moving" brought eyes back to the south. Indians materialized from places it seemed they could not have been and scurried back to the safety of the stream bank. The appearance of the newcomers had taken the Indians by surprise also and they were regrouping to study the situation. Even from that far distance Jase could see these Indians were from another tribe and could even be enemies of the attacking tribe. That thought gave Jase little hope though as reports were becoming all the more common of former enemy tribes banding together against the whites.

All was quiet for about thirty minutes while all parties surveyed each other. Looking through the telescope at the newcomers Jase was surprised to spot the Sioux he knew as Army Coat. The Sioux moved closer and more toward the east where they had an open view of both the wagons and the stream bed where the Shoshoni were. Jase, remembering Army Coat signing that he would remember Jase and that they would fight no more, stepped outside the wagon circle to the north and moved a few paces toward the Sioux. He hoped the big Indian would indeed recognize him and hold to his promise.

Army Coat rode some distance toward him gesturing back some other braves that started to follow. He sat his horse some distance out and studied Jase for a minute. Pointing two fingers at his own eyes then a single finger at Jase he turned and rode back to his people. Jase turned back to the wagons. He knew only that Army Coat recognized him but had no idea what his intentions might be. Staying out of normal rifle range from the wagons, Army coat and two others rode east and then south toward the creek. Stopping some distance from the creek, Army Coat stuck his lance in the ground and they waited.

Shortly, three of the Shoshoni rode out to join them. Jase watched the meeting through his telescope.

At first the meeting seemed cordial enough, and then one of the Shoshonis became quite excited using much sign and gesturing toward the west. Some of the gestures appeared to be aimed at the wagons, but most seemed more toward the general direction. Jase was able to read some of the sign and picked up some of the key meanings. Whites, soldiers, family, death, and anguish were the main focuses of the Shoshoni. One thing that was very evident was that he wanted all whites dead.

Army Coat talked a bit gesturing toward the large group on the hill. The Shoshonis seemed upset by this and they talked a little longer. Army coat pointed to the Shoshoni, held up one finger, and pointed toward the wagons. The Shoshonis all nodded and then the angry one made sign for "we fight" toward the wagons and the three turned and rode back to the stream bed. Army Coat pulled his lance from the ground and he and the others rode back to the group on the hill.

The Indians talked for a while then Army coat rode about halfway to the wagons before stopping and again thrusting his lance into the ground. He pointed at Jase, jumped off his horse and sat cross legged on the ground. The rest of the Sioux split into three groups and began moving around the wagons. By the time Jase had mounted The Black and rode to where Army Coat sat on the ground they had started to make three camps. One to the east of the wagons, one to the west of the wagons, and one between the wagons and those in the stream.

Army Coat rose as Jase dismounted and said "It is good to see the white warrior with the crooked arm and strong medicine again" as he held out his arm. Jase smiled, took the man's extended hand and said "It is good to see you also, as long as we do not fight." The Sioux laughed and said "I have said we would not and we will not." "When we first met you gave me not only the gift of the buffalo but that of my own life" he continued. "When the buffalo fell I knew your big gun could have easily reached me" adding "Even though I was trying to take your life, you did not take mine." "Whites had killed much of my family and many others of my people" he explained, "My hatred was great and I wished to see all whites dead." "Our meeting helped me to realize that not all whites are like those that kill our people, but the Shoshoni has not found that out, he added pointing toward the creek."

"Whites attacked his people while they camped on the river of the Bear." "They killed many of his people and destroyed their food and belongings." "Because of that many of those that escaped died before spring because of lack of food and shelter." "He watched his wife and baby son die in this way so his hatred is understandable." "I have told the Shoshoni that you are a friend, but his heart is dark and he vows to fight even if we would join you." "He says this even knowing that fighting us alone they could not win." "Many would die and there would be much more sorrow." Jase agreed and said "My people wish no one any harm, but will defend ourselves at all costs." Jase asked Army Coat if he thought the other warriors could change the Shoshoni's mind if they knew they were entering a battle they could not win. Army Coat said he did not think they would even try. All had suffered great loss and were in low spirits thus death was not a thing for them to fear.

Army Coat lowered his head then straightened and looked Jase in the eye. "There may be one way to avoid the fight" he said, "but I don't know for sure." As Jase started to ask what it might be, Army Coat held up his hand to stop him and continued. "You are a fearless warrior and show great skill with your guns." "Your medicine is strong" he said pointing at the medallion, "and I know you have heart and will fight until you have nothing to fight with." He paused still holding his hand up for silence, then continued. "I know you have one arm that is not as it was at birth so I must ask how well you fight with these" he said pointing to the tomahawk and knife on Jase's belt. A slight grin crossed Jase's face and after some thought he answered "At one time I fought well, now I do not know, why do you ask?" "When talking to the Shoshoni I said words that led him to believe I doubted his ability in hand to hand combat with a white warrior" Army coat said. With a solemn look at Jase he continued, "I do not think his pride would allow him to turn down a direct challenge, and his warriors would be bound by what was agreed upon."

Jase thought a moment then asked, "Do you think he would agree to let the others go no matter what the outcome, even if I lose?" Army Coat pondered the question, then answered "Yes, most are not white and my braves will fight to protect those you care about." "I will make this known and I believe those with him will force him to accept the terms, if he accepts the challenge." Readily

Jase stated, "Take the challenge to him and do your best to persuade him to take it with those terms." "Just he and I with hawk and knife" thinking a second he added "and lance if he wishes."

"You have a lance?" Army Coat asked. "No" Jase answered, "but I can make one that will do what I need it to do". Army Coat pulled his lance from the ground and held it out to Jase. "Use mine" he grunted, "It is a strong one". Jase accept the lance, hefted it and moved it around some before answering, "It is a good, strong lance, but I may have to make some change with it if I were to use it so I thank you for your offer, but should build one according to my needs." Army coat refused the lance as Jase attempted to hand it back stating, "No, it is yours now, put your medicine on it as you wish, I will talk with the Shoshoni." With that he jumped on his stocky pony and rode around the wagons to the camp between them and the Shoshoni.

Jase went back to the wagons and told the others what had been said. He explained that the Sioux would see that no harm came to them regardless of the outcome of the fight. Upon mention of the challenge, two of the former slaves requested to take Jake's place. Both were quite good with their fists and wrestling, and perhaps even with a knife. Neither had experience with a tomahawk or lance though and both knew their chance of surviving such a fight was slim to none. The knowledge that both were willing to give up their life for his caused Jase to smile. He thanked them and explained that the fight had to be with the white man as that was where the Shoshoni's hatred was aimed.

The sun was getting low in the western sky before Army coat rode to a spot between the wagons and his camp and dismounted. Jase walked the distance to meet him. As Jase walked up, Army Coat extended his hand and said, "It is done, your terms are met." "My people will see to it that the promises are kept" he added. "Tomorrow when the sun reaches half way between the hills and straight above you must be at our camp" adding, "You may have three with you, the Shoshoni will have three with him, however none are to interfere." "Agreed" Jase answered, "Thank you my friend, you have proven to be more than true to your word." A slight smile crossed the Sioux's face as he extended his hand and said "Fight well my brother; your death would bring me sadness." With that he turned away and walked his pony back to his camp. As Jase walked back to the wagons, he reached up and touched the medallion that hung around his neck. "Well old friend," he said aloud to Jake's spirit, "You taught me well, I hope I can make you proud."

Though Jase had studied Army Coat's well built lance, he had held off making any changes to it until he was sure he would need it. Now, with the challenge accepted, he set about making some changes to better fit it for the style of shaft fighting Jake had taught him. The stout shaft was tipped on one end with what appeared to be the business end of an army saber about five inches long lashed tightly into a split in the shaft by rawhide. Jase could not help but notice the traces of blood stains on the rawhide and shaft. "It looks like you have served our Sioux friend well" he murmured as he continued to study the lance. He started to remove the three eagle feathers that hung from the other end but thought better of it. Twirling the lance and making other moves with it he decided he needed to shorten it by about a foot and a half.

That was the change he had waited to make. With the help of Josiah, one of the Negros that had offered to fight for him, he cut the shaft to the desired length. While Josiah shaped the end of the lance to Jase's specifications, Jase removed the handle he had made for the old axe head he had acquired while a prisoner; replacing it with the end of the lance they had cut off. Jase then carved a likeness of the six peddled flower from the necklace part of his medallion into the new handle. Leaving the Eagle feathers fastened to the end, the heavy tomahawk was complete. That work completed, Jase turned his attention to the light tomahawk he intended to use in battle the next day.

He carved four of the flower designs into the handle placing them with care. He left the high points of the carvings rough to aid with his grip so the hawk would not slip in a sweaty hand. He then took a well worn rock from his belongings and worked on the cutting edge. It was much after dark and most of the camp had retired before Jase was satisfied with the edge which now matched that of his knife. He and Pricilla had talked while he worked, and now hand in hand they headed to their bed which was under one of the wagons and surrounded with canvas.

Jase could hear others stirring when he awoke with the sun. After greeting the others that were up, he took a cup of coffee from the pot that sat next to the fire and walked to a place outside the circle of wagons. Sipping the coffee, he set about preparing his mind and body for the fight that was to come. While he slowly stretched his muscles to rid them of any tightness his mind worked on the challenge that lay ahead.

He knew little about his opponent other than that he was about a head taller and out weighted Jase by fifty or more pounds. He had determined that as he had watched the brave and Army Coat when they first talked. This he decided would give the brave the advantage of a longer reach and perhaps a bit more strength. A slight smile crossed Jase's features as he realized that Jake had also had the advantage of reach over him during his training. The narrow point between full contact and distant battle that he would have to avoid to lessen the Indian's advantage should be almost inbred by his training. As Jase began to dwell on the mental aspects of the fight he began to feel that the advantage there might be his.

The Brave would be driven by his hatred and desire to kill, whereas Jase would be driven by a desire to live and protect his friends. A person driven by hatred has a tendency to forge ahead toward their goal of harm to the object of that hatred. Skill acquired by past experience and training will guide their advance toward that goal. However, the stronger the focus on their hatred the less attention will be paid to experience and training. Thus, the more apt they are to make errors.

Fear also can hinder a person's abilities as their focus narrows on escape from the object of their fear. This is why many humans and animals become victims with little or no resistance. However, in some cases, both human and animal, where there is no chance to rid themselves of the danger, the desire to live or escape builds a strength that allows them to overcome far more than their normal abilities could accomplish. The war had almost totally deadened the emotion of fear in Jase, but finding Pricilla again sparked a very strong desire to live. Also, he was in a position where he could not avoid the fight. He intended to win.

Jase limped slightly from the bullet wound in his right leg, but it was almost too full strength though just a little tight. He did not feel it would present any problem, but knew that the limp would be noticed by the Indian and perhaps looked on as a weak point. Jase was sure that the Brave would consider his scared and crooked left arm to be a point of weakness, and to a point, it was. That would mean that at least some of the Indian's efforts would be focused there. A bit of knowledge that could be used to Jase's advantage. Adding to this was the fact that Jase had acquired a reasonable bit of knowledge about the fighting styles of various Indians, but much of what Jake had taught him came from other lands and would seem strange to the Indian. Pondering these things, Jase felt that he fairly well knew what actions the Indian might take and what actions he would have apply in order to win. He gave no thought to loosing. He would not leave Pricilla alone again. He had to win so they could continue their life together. He fingered the Medallion as he walked back to camp remembering the things the Old Man had taught him.

Jase ate lightly and drank some tea he had made from the herbs he carried with him. He sat relaxed talking with the others until the sun had been up about three hours. He got up, stretched some more, then pulling the lance from the ground he started toward Army Coat's camp. Though he had asked them to stay, Burl, Ira, and Pricilla refused and walked with him. Ira carried the heavy tomahawk Jase had made the night before. The others stayed with the wagons in case anything went awry.

Army Coat's camp was setup around a

circle about forty feet across. As Jase and his group came to the edge of the camp, they could see the Shoshonis hurrying to get to the other side. The Shoshoni did not want to be the last to arrive as that could be taken as a sign of fear. He had four other braves with him and was bolstering his courage by telling them how he was going to kill this white man and avenge his family.

Jase understood enough of the language to comprehend what was said. As he took the LeMat from his belt and handed it to Pricilla, he turned to the Brave. Using as good of Shoshoni as he could muster and using sign to help he said, "I am sorry that whites have killed your family and friends, and I am also sorry that you have picked today to die." Jase then removed his shirt to indicate that he was ready. The Shoshoni's anger flared and he screamed at Jase telling him that he would be the one to die.

Army Coat and another brave stood in the center of the circle with Jase and The Shoshoni standing on the outside opposite each other. The Shoshoni was stripped to only a loin cloth and moccasins. The moccasins were beaded with designs depicting speed and strength. In his belt was a bone handled knife and he held his long lance in his right hand. The French made tomahawk he carried in his left hand was of a design used primarily by eastern Indians and seldom seen in the western tribes. The upward thrust of the blade point made it a very formable weapon, but put some limits on its use in close quarters. Jase took note of this.

Jase wore leather britches, well worn moccasins, and Jake's Medallion. He carried only the shortened lance in his hands with his light tomahawk and knife still in his belt. The scars and crookedness of his arm were quite visible without his shirt. As Jase and the Shoshoni studied each other across the circle, Jase could see the brave's eyes shift and hold on that sign of weakness momentarily. As Army Coat and the other brave stated the term of the fight, Jase again caught the Shoshoni showing interest in that possible limitation. Both fighters nodded acceptance of the terms and the two speakers moved from the circle.

The Shoshoni began circling to Jase's left while slowly starting to advance. Jase stepped out straight toward him and began to slowly twirl the lance in his hands. Neither the non-circling advance nor the twirling of the lance were familiar tactics to the Indian and Jase saw a brief flash of confusion in his eyes. The Indian made a couple of test thrusts with his lance that were easily deflected by the spin of Jase's. He then stepped into a lightning thrust aimed at Jase's hands at the center of the twirling object.

Jase dropped his body down and away from the advancing spear point, while his own lance snaked out with the added momentum of the spin. The butt end of Jase's lance smacked solidly on the ankle of the Indian's leading foot as he stepped into the thrust. The foot was knocked sideways just as the weight was coming down on it and the big Indian hit the ground hard. Jase spun the lance around and thrust the sharp point at the Indian's body as he was moving quickly off the ground. The Indian was fast, too fast. He pared Jase's thrust away with his tomahawk as he moved up and away from Jase.

The brief encounter brought grunts and shouts of approval from the onlookers, which added to the anger showing in the eyes of the Indian. However, the Indian moved with a visible limp and more wariness as he realized that the death of this white man with the bad arm was not going to come as easily as he had anticipated. He even gave some ground as Jase advanced with the again spinning lance.

Jase gave no ground other than keeping out of the reach of the tomahawk in the

Indian's hand. Both thrust and parried, but neither could so much as touch the other with their lance's lethal points. The Indian would work toward Jase's left and Jase would counter move to keep the Indian always in front of him. Suddenly, the Indian threw his lance at Jase's midsection and followed it in with his swinging tomahawk.

The unexpected move caught Jase off guard and as he moved to his right to clear the lance that was deflected off his own, he moved almost directly into the path of the swinging tomahawk. An upward sweep of his lance deflected the tomahawk from a direct hit into his side, but had the added effect of knocking the lance from his grip. A solid straight punch to the Indian's nose, delivered by his left hand, set the Indian back on his heels and partially blinded him for a moment. Jase grabbed his knife from its sheath as he spun away from the Indian.

Jase was aware of a burning pain in his side, and the dampness of blood working its way behind his belt. Jase did not think the cut was deep, but was well aware of how close he had come to the fight being over. Realizing he had felt no pain in his left arm as it delivered the solid punch, he trusted it to slide the tomahawk from his belt just in time to meet a swinging rush by the Indian. Jase ducked the swinging tomahawk that narrowly missed his head as he spun on his right foot while kicking the Indian behind one knee with the heal of his left. Continuing the spin with a backward swing of his tomahawk Jase felt the hawk slice deep into the Indian's shoulder. As the Indian tried to move away, Jase caught him with an elbow between the shoulder blades. The Indian went down face first.

Jase followed him to the ground with a knee in his back and his knife at the Indian's throat. Holding the knife at the Indian's throat hard enough to cause a trickle of blood Jase said "I will let you live, but no more fight, --- agreed?" An older Shoshoni that had come with the Indian translated and the Indian spoke and slightly nodded his agreement. Jase looked to Army Coat and after receiving an agreeing nod from him he gained his feet, turned and walked toward Pricilla.

He saw her eyes widen and saw her start to raise the heavy LeMat. He sprang to his left swinging both tomahawk and knife as he turned just as the loud boom of two rifles sounded much as one. He saw the Indian, knife upraised, literally knocked through the air by two heavy bullets at close range. Both Army Coat and the old Shoshoni that had translated Jase's words held smoking rifles pointed at where the Indian had been.

The Shoshoni looked at Jase with sad eyes and stated "It would have been better you had killed him." "We agreed, enough fight," he added before he turned away. The Shoshonis then gathered up the body of the dead Indian and walked back to the stream bed. "The old man was his uncle" Army Coat said when they had left, "They will bother you no more."

Jase thanked Army Coat for all he had done. He then took the heavy tomahawk from Ira and presented it to him as a gift telling him that the carving he had added represented the power that flows outward from each man. Army Coat took the gift with only a nod, but when Jase tried to return the borrowed lance he stated "It carries your medicine now, it is yours." As Jase put his arm around Pricilla and started to leave, Army Coat stopped him. He handed Jase a small black rock that had been carved into the shape of a bear. "Take this with you," he said, "You may return it when we meet again, as I feel it will happen." "We go to the lands beyond the Big Horns by where we first met," he added "Perhaps you will find yourself there again."

The Shoshonis filed south out of the stream bed with the bodies of the brave Jase had fought and nine others draped over their horses. They would lay them to rest in a place where whites did not travel. After they had gone, Army Coat gave a wave and he and his band disappeared over a rise to the north east. As the last Indian went out of sight, Ira gave a shout and cracked his whip over the heads of the horses pulling the lead wagon and they started toward the Green River.

Due to the lateness of the year, the Green was an easy ford and they made good time before an early snow hit them about two days out of Fort Bridger. The clay soil become slick yet stuck to boots, wheels, and hooves making travel almost impossible. It was four days before the intermittent rain and snow stopped and it was dry enough for decent travel. The temperature dropped to a point where the warmth of the fires was more a necessity than a comfort. Fort Bridger was a welcome sight when they finally arrived.

W. C. Dick

Chapter 13

The winter was spent in the relative safety and comfort of Fort Bridger. During breaks in the weather, Jase and some of the others at the fort would scout the area for some miles around. Though much different from the climate and terrain most were used to in the East, there was some area around the fort that showed good promise. One valley that was fed by a stream originating from the mountains to the South caught Jase's eye. It was big country, and Jase picked that small part of it to build a new life for he and Pricilla.

He began buying and trading for any seed that he could acquire and whatever livestock that looked good. He even hired four men that had come up from Texas to work the cattle he acquired. The cowboys agreed to work the stock through the rest of the winter, and until the end of summer, but intended to head south "before the snow hits the high peaks next fall." Jase knew horses well, but the cattle were new to him, however he felt he could learn enough to work them by the time the cowboys left.

Burl's smoke burned lungs did not make

it through the winter and he died before the thaw. Because of their respect for him, his former slaves used pick and shovel to dig a grave for him in the frozen ground. He was buried high on a hill, facing east toward the burnt out plantation they all loved. It was marked with a wooden cross that Ira built from the wood of one of the wagons. The wood he used had been taken from the main house to repair the wagon before they started their journey. Burl did however live long enough for Pricilla to inform him that he was going to be a Grandfather.

In the spring Jase was anxious to start up the valley he had chosen. Pricilla was showing with child, and he wanted to have a house built for her before the baby was born. They moved the livestock up first and built holding pens for them. They then took enough supplies to build two sod and wood buildings. One would be Jase and Pricilla's home and the other one would be for the men.

The third trip while moving most of the supplies and personal belongings the runoff from the mountain had the creek running heavily and rain there had set in. Two of the three wagons became mired down in the mud to the point where they had to be lightened in order to continue on. About half of the supplies had to be unloaded to the high side of the creek in order to free the wagons. The men were coated with mud by the time they got the wagons free and they still had a rough, muddy trail ahead. Covering the pile of supplies as best they could, they took the rest on to the homestead.

They were almost through unloading the supplies left on the wagons when Jase realized the medallion was not around his neck. Thinking back he vaguely remembered a tug on his neck as they struggled to get the last wagon up the bank. Though the tug was slight, it had been enough to pull him of balance and almost under the wheel of the wagon. It was perhaps good the medallion had come loose.

Barking Coyote watched from the clump of boulders high on the hill as the whites struggled with the wagons. The antelope skin he was using to keep most of the rain off came from the antelope he had killed two weeks ago. It had supplied all that he and his little band had to eat for quite some time and it had been gone three days now. His empty stomach growled as he watched from his vantage point.

He watched as the men moved off leaving part of their load on the bank. He knew there was food in the pile that was left as he had seen it as they were unloading. His people needed food and there was some for the taking. As soon as he felt the men had traveled far enough so he would not be seen, he led his small band down the hill to the needed supplies.

Barking Coyote cautioned his people to take only what they needed and could carry. He hoped that by taking only a small amount the whites would not follow them to get their supplies back. If they were followed, the Indians, mostly women and children, had little to defend themselves with and life had taught him that the whites would show no mercy. He had these thoughts on his mind when he saw the splash of blue protruding out of the mud part way down the bank.

Sliding down the bank he pulled the blue stones from the mud. Wiping the mud off as best he could the young man was intrigued with the medallion. At the least, the stones would make good trading material. Perhaps, finding this after finding food for his people might mean it is a good sign. Folding the necklace into the pouch that hung around his neck, he clawed his way up the bank. Putting the cover back on the pile after they gathered what food and blankets they could carry, the Indians moved quickly up the hill opposite the one they had come down.

The next day, after the rain quit, Jase and his men took two wagons and went after the remaining supplies. Jase watched for the medallion while they loaded the supplies, but did not see it so he began to look around. However, it was not until one of the men commented that there seemed to be more supplies when they were moving them up the bank than they were loading now, that an actual check was made. Deciding that the supplies were short, they all studied the area for clues to the missing goods.

One of Jase's men was the one that spotted the moccasin tracks. A close look at the rain washed area revealed parts of moccasin tracks and an impression left by a hand digging something out of the mud. Jase knew that the Medallion was gone. Working in ever widening circles, enough of the tracks were found to tell part of the story. A small band of Indians, mostly women and children, had found the medallion, taken food and blankets, and left the area by going over the hill to the east.

Jase's men asked about going after the Indians, but Jase answered them by looking up the hill and speaking out loud. "I hope what you took helps you on your journey" he said. Then added, as he touched his chest where the medallion used to rest, "May Jake's medicine help you protect you and yours as it helped me." Turning to the rest, he said "let's go home."

After unloading the remaining supplies at the homestead, Jase, Ira, and one of the cowboys took the three wagons back to Fort Bridger. Ira and Josiah asked to stay and work for Jase and Pricilla and were gladly accepted. The rest of the former slaves and the two men from Oregon elected to traverse on toward California. One of the wagons was loaded with supplies to replace those taken by the Indians and the other two were given to those heading west.

Good-bys were said and Jase's small group headed to their new home. Ira sat contentedly on the seat of the wagon listening to the crate of chickens cackle in the wagon bed behind him. He followed Josiah and the cowboy as they drove several head of horses up the trail. Ahead of them he could see Jase on the Black holding hands with Pricilla as she rode alongside him. He began singing a song he used to sing in the happy days back on the plantation.

Miles away, in the war torn east, a group of men met in a secluded room. The speaker was saying "We have to build a railroad to

California to transport the gold from there to help with the war effort." "There will be those that will oppose us and much will be needed," another said. "We will have the government behind us" the speaker said, "and we will take what we need."

GPS Coordinate Gathering

Louis L'Amour stated he had been to the places he wrote a description of in his books. So, one day I decided to try to trace some of the travels described in a couple of his books. Using his descriptions along with my knowledge of the areas in which they took place, I feel I was able to follow quite closely what he had written about. I enjoyed the challenge and being able to see what his eyes had seen. That is one of the reasons I elected to include a guide for others to follow where I had been as I wrote this book.

I had a rough draft of the book written and had visited most of the areas I wanted to use that were located in Wyoming before I acquired a GPS and started collecting coordinates. As I do most of my traveling by motorcycle it was very enjoyable to visit the various locations again and collect the information needed. Then I loaded the bike and headed east to try and find the location I had envisioned for the boyhood home of my main character. Also, though I have studied quite a bit about the Civil War, I wanted to visit numerous sites and try to get a feel for them and those embattled there.

When I left, I knew the approximate area I felt Jase might have grown up in, the unit he might have served in and its history, and the general route he needed to take to be true to the book. Using those things as guidelines, I just followed the front wheel over whatever route seemed right at the time. That route led me through some battlefield sites and eventually to the area in which I had envisioned Jase's house to be. Believe it or not, I floated along back roads over hills and valleys looking for a house that met the description I had in my mind. I came down a hill; found an intersection at the bottom and for no particular reason took the road that took off to the right. A couple of curves later I spotted a house similar to what I had envisioned and I had found Jase's house. You will have to find it with GPS if you wish to be there.

I could not find a town in the vicinity to use for the town where he met Pricilla, as I could not find any that were there at the time the book depicts. Big Shanty was an interesting visit and the GPS point will have you in front of a court house that stands on land that was Camp McDonald. From there, as you travel north to the corn field, there are many battle sites to visit and learn from. As I walked the ground that had been so heavily soaked with blood so many years ago, I found a large rock that was about even with the ground. If you stand on the coordinates for the cornfield, look around and you should see that rock where I envisioned both wounded and dead laying.

The maps I had of the prison showed only a stone building and a cemetery left. Try as I might I could not locate the building before I found a local who informed me that the building had been burnt and torn down a couple of years before. That left the resting place of many of those that died there as the GPS point for the prison. From there I drifted the back roads to the Northwest looking for the shelter, and the place Jase met the union soldier. I found both that came very close to what I was seeing in my mind's eye.

From there I headed toward Fort Ridgley. Traveling paths that might well have been used in those days I found many places Jase might have come on the wrecked wagon so I invite any who might travel that way to look and see what they might see. While studying the history and area around Fort Ridgley I found much of interest though very little of it made it into the book.

White Stone, in North Dakota, has memorials to both soldiers and Indians, but the differences in them says a lot about the feelings of our government and many others. If you would travel from there to Lake DeSmett, as I hope some will do, you will find that there are many routes you might follow. I might suggest one that would take you through the beautiful Black Hills of South Dakota. Perhaps by being there you might understand why the various tribes held this area as sacred.

From Lake DeSmett there are two main routes over the Big Horn Mountains. I chose the Southern route through Tensleep, which is listed. However you might prefer the Northern route which would take you by the Medicine Wheel that was mentioned in the book. Either way you can end up with a good soak in the mineral waters at Thermopolis.

The rise and sinks of the Popoagie River are easily reached by car, but if one is able bodied enough the two mile hike to the falls and the climb would be highly recommended. From the parking lot for the falls one can either go back around by the paved road or over the top on the dirt road to reach the historical area of South Pass.

Although I have ridden most of the Oregon/Mormon trails in this area I had not actually visited South pass Station as it was on private property. When I asked and received permission to visit the site I was privileged to take a picture and floor plans of the station that I had found in my research with me. This was the first time the owners had actually seen what the fallen down structure there actually looked like at the time of its use. The battle there in the book depicts these images.

If one stops at the Indian fight site and the Green River ford and one lets the mind wander perhaps you could visualize the scene my writing depicts. As one walks the grounds of Fort Bridger it is easily visualized as the bustling activity center it was in those days. From there you have to follow the old railroad bed past the creek crossing to the place they called home. It is easily found as there are some coke kilns that were put there in later years before the rail moved from there to its present route.

If you elect to follow even part of these travels, or locate these sites using one of the mapping sites on your computer, such as google, I hope you find even a small amount of the enjoyment I found as I wrote this story.

Happy trails, Wayne Dick

GPS Points for book

House	N 35 10.880'	W	82 56.994'
Big Shanty (Camp McDonald)	N 34 01.408' W 84 37.009'		
Cornfield	N 39 28.989'	W	77 44.803'
Prison	N 39 56.628'	W.	83 04.560'
First shelter	N 39 56.819'	W	83 15.202'
Union Soldier	N 40 04.125'	W	83 37.493'
Fort Ridgley	N 44 27.176'	W	94 44.064'
White Stone	N 46 10.124'	W	98 51.410'
Lake De Smett	N 44 30.289'	W 106	47.078'
Tensleep	N 44 01.798'	W	107 27.068'
Thermopolis	N 43 39.280'	W 108	11.659'
Rise	N 42 45.137'	W	108 48.149'
Sinks	N 42 44.900'	W	108 48.554'
Falls (top)	N 42 43.203'	W	108 52.970'

Burnt Ranch (South Pass Station)N 42 22.617'
    W 108 43.102'

Indian Fight   N 41 57.402'   W   109
41.526'

Ford, Green River   N 41 52.106'   W 109
47.458'

Fort Bridger   N 41 19.088'   W   110
23.385'

Creek Crossing   N41 15.741'W 110 36.490'

Home   N 41 13.120'   W   110
37.324'

Made in the USA
Charleston, SC
06 March 2016